Dragons AND WITCHES

FAIRY TALE VILLAINS REIMAGINED

Susan Bianculli   Sarah Lyn Eaton
Ariane Felix   J.G. Formato
Valerie Hunter   Mari Mancusi
Kath Boyd Marsh   Joy Preble
C.H. Spalding   Renee Whittington

CBaY Books
Dallas, Texas

Dragons and Witches:
Fairy Tale Villains Reimagined
Edited by Madeline Smoot

For more information, write:
CBAY Books
PO Box 670296
Dallas, TX 75367

Children's Brains are Yummy Books
Dallas, Texas
www.cbaybooks.com

ISBN: 978-1-933767-61-1
eBook ISBN: 978-1-933767-62-8
Kindle ISBN: 978-1-933767-63-5
PDF ISBN: 978-1-933767-64-2

Table of Contents

Burning
C.H. Spalding

I woke to pain.

Pain is holy. It purifies us, relieves us of our sin. When I am grown, my pain will always tear through my body, a symphony of sensation to remind me to focus on the greater good. I am young and have only known the training pain that slowly prepares us for the inward changes when the spikes that rise from our bodies will also pierce us within.

I opened my eyes, saw the wreckage within my escape pod. The world outside was bright and green, loud with a cacophony of voices from abominations. This planet must be new to my people, or we would already have killed them all, all the birds and mammals, and any reptiles longer than the span of my front claws. Insects we usually left alive, and the seas are irredeemable depths of poison sin that not even our fire can cleanse.

My claws hit the controls, sounds alerting me to their status. My beacon had been in a part of my pod that had broken off; it was active, but I would need to

1

get to it to send an actual message. There were no signs that other pods had reached this planet when the ship hull burst. I was alone for now. Perhaps for the rest of my life.

My middle left leg was dislocated, and I pulled it back into position. If it did not heal correctly, I would have to amputate, but not yet. The planet had plenty of nitrogen and hydrogen in its atmosphere, and there is little carbon based that my people can't digest. I could reasonably expect to survive here, long enough to wait for rescue and to choose my path if it did not come.

The pod was crushed badly. If I'd been full-grown, I would have had to leave limbs behind to leave at all, but I had only recently had my full naming. My exo-skeleton was scratched and dented in places but not breached. I worked to keep it that way as I flipped upside down and clung to the wall and scurried out the broken view port.

The world outside was worse than I had imagined. Dozens of winged creatures took to the air as I emerged, and a herd of small herbivores startled and ran. There was profligate life everywhere I looked. I could work my whole life and not make a dent in it.

I caught a snake from a nearby tree in my jaw and

devoured it, more because I needed the protein than that I had already begun my hopeless, holy work. If my people came and found me, we would work together to consecrate this world. If not …

The sensors around my ears allowed me to triangulate on the beacon. In a civilized world, with food contained to vats, it would have been a brief journey. Through this wilderness it could take days.

I slithered through the underbrush as best I could, using my limbs to clear obstacles. The herbivores startled at my approach, and I hadn't the time or the energy to waste in chasing them down. There would be time for hunting later.

The trees formed a canopy overhead, which thinned the growth a little on the ground. It was my first wild world, and I fell into a rhythm that turned to enjoyment—over, under, beside, and onward towards my goal.

Pleasure, of course, is a sin, and it was the highest grace that mine was ended.

The sky opened up in front of me, and I pulled myself to a stop with the help of all six limbs. The green forest ended, and in front of me was only water.

We are the children of fire and blood. We are stronger than pain. From infancy we can squirm through fire unharmed. Falls rarely kill us, and we can continue with all limbs gone. If we live long enough, lost limbs will grow back. Our death is usually inherent in our bodies; we burn out from our own fire or are torn apart from within. Water is less our foe than the absence of what we are. Our fire cannot burn in it. Our bodies cannot take in nitrogen and hydrogen from it. Our exoskeletons do not allow us to stay atop it.

The water in front of me extended beyond the limits of my sight. If there was a land bridge across, it too lay beyond the limits of my sight, either to North or to South. Since the beacon still worked, it had to be on dry land, but it would have been far easier to cross the vacuum of space than the poison depths in front of me.

I threw objects in to try to assess the depth. Stones fell, wood floated, and the small mammal I flung in could swim. It was at least three times my length deep, and it likely got deeper as it went further from shore.

I shrugged my limbs back in against my body. I could think as I went, and one direction was as promising as the other. I headed North.

In that first despair, I would have been tempted to make my choice without thought, just to burn everything in my path. I was too young for fire, just as I was too young for blood. I had to grow to full size, grow to the time of my choice. Instead I continued to slither north. As rescue grew more unlikely I ate more of the creatures I encountered.

The sun set and a trio of moons rose, shifting light that was enough for my purposes. By the time the sun rose again the beacon was becoming faint, and I reluctantly turned back. There was still no sign of a way across.

I slowed a little on my way back, cooling my thoughts. If I were a mammal, I might be able to swim. If I were made of wood, I could float across if the wind and water let me.

Back at my starting place I paused and considered, then set about gathering what I needed.

The first time I threw a small mammal at a floating piece of wood I missed, and it drowned. The second time I threw too hard, and either killed it or knocked it unconscious against the wood. Either way, it drowned. The third time, the animal reached the wood and scrabbled aboard but, once there, was helpless to control the movement of the branch.

I used different sizes of wood, different animals to fling after them. Most just held on as the wind and water carried them ... somewhere. Eventually one clever creature clung to the wood while kicking at the water with its feet as though steering. I was so impressed that I hesitated to kill it when it returned to shore. That moment was all it needed to escape, and I accepted this sin with my others. Mercy is a great weakness.

I calculated as best I could, then pulled a fallen tree to the edge of the water. I grabbed hold with my front claws and pushed off with the back ones. The tree trunk rolled in the water, and I scrambled to stay afloat. Dying like this would not cleanse my sins.

There would be glory for my people if I succeeded in my quest. My head would join the ancestors in the Hall of the Exalted if this crossing led to my rescue and the taming of this world.

I let this thought warm me as I headed out into the endless sea.

Some creatures sleep, but my kind does not. We may reach a place of reverie or contemplation, but we remain aware and in control of mind and body. It was a day later when I at last followed the beacon to shore. My claws pushed against stone below the water, and I hauled the tree trunk with me up onto dry land.

The beacon was close now, and I looked for signs of it even as I caught a bird between my jaws, then another in my front claws. My carapace was itching, certain sign that I was growing.

At last I found the beacon on the forest floor, lit by the hole it had rent in the canopy above. I opened it carefully with front claws and teeth, then activated its sensors.

The beacon's range was far more than my headset, but there was no other energy signature on this planet or in the space around it. I was truly alone. I thrummed my breath to calm myself, then set the beacon to record my message.

"This is Ez-Kotii of the 192nd cohort. This world is ripe with abomination, and no others of our kind are here. Let the histories show that I crossed a day's journey of water upon a fallen tree to reach this place. I will grow, and I will seek to cleanse this place. I choose ..." My voice faltered for just a moment, and I hit pause. One fire breather could never clear this planet. There really only was one choice. I resumed recording. "I choose the path of blood."

I set the beacon to broadcast. I would grow, and when the spines pierced me internally as well as extending from my body, I would set my body to carrying life instead of fire. I would nurture my body so that perhaps fifteen, perhaps twenty young would devour me from within on their way out into the world. There would be no one to teach them, only their hunger and later their pain. They would learn. It is what our kind does.

I allowed myself a moment to accept it and then turned back to the forest. It was time to hunt.

The survey ship shifted into the system and took up a distant orbit around the yellow sun. The ensign on Comm alerted the ship's captain—only a lieutenant, officially—at the energy signature coming from the second planet, a promising looking world with three moons.

"Audio," the captain ordered, leaning back into her chair. One of the grav-strap buckles dug into her shoulder. It would have to be adjusted. She'd been around, had seen plenty of things, in her years in the service.

But she wasn't used to having this seat. Yet.

The ensign had complied. Momentarily a rasping, hissing, musical sound filled the bridge, a minor key in quarter tones.

"It's old," the ensign said. "A century, at least. Are we going down?"

The captain shook her head. "Not when you hear that. Never when you hear that."

The ensign blinked in surprise, looking up from his controls. "Do you know what it means?"

"Close enough." The captain checked her sensors; land-based animals were severely limited on the planet, although the seas teemed with life. "It means, 'Here Be Dragons.'"

C.H Spalding has been writing since the 80's, though only dared make submissions professionally in the last few years. Most of those published have been in science fiction or fantasy, and currently there are several young adult novels sitting around unfinished. Spare time is usually taken up by children, pets, artwork, and watching too many documentaries on YouTube.

A Very Baba Yaga Halloween
Joy Preble

Baba Yaga sat by the fire in her hut in the forest. The flames heated her ancient bones as she rocked and dreamed and planned, her iron teeth glinting in the fire-light. On her lap, her huge hands rested, gnarled fingers twining. When she desired hot sweet tea to quench her thirst, one hand detached from her wrist and scuttled down her leg to the floor, thick nails clattering on the wood as it went to fetch her drink.

It was nice to be a witch. Nice to have the power. Occasionally a too thin child stuck between her teeth. But why quibble? She was Baba Yaga. These things sometimes happened.

Underneath the hut, two enormous chicken legs scrabbled the earth, carrying her house this way and that. No predators could find the mighty Baba Yaga unless she willed it to be. Lost boys and girls might stumble upon her, but everyone knew what happened to them. Eaten. Ground to dust in the witch's mortar, crushed into nothingness by the same pestle with which she stirred the air as she flew.

The wise Death Goddess. The Bone Mother.

Today, though, a small worry gnawed at her like she would often gnaw a stray child's leg bone. Halloween was coming. All Hallow's Eve. The night that spirits rose and walked the earth and things that went bump in the night showed themselves as solid and real as the humans who ran from them.

"Do not worry, Mistress," her three horsemen—one red, one black, one white—told her. "You are the mighty Baba Yaga. The Wild Crone. You hold dominion over all. What is one silly night? Foolish humans dressed in foolish costumes, pretending to be something they are not. Bah!"

It *was* a silly holiday, she agreed. But something in the horsemen's words stuck with her anyway. Baba Yaga had never appeared as anything but herself. She tapped her huge chin with one enormous hand. *What would it hurt, if for one night, she became something else?*

The thought careened through her brain as thoughts sometimes do.

Yes. She would do it.

From under her rocking chair by the fire, her cat

mewed loudly, threading its way around the scrape of her roughened ankles. In the fire, the bones of the lost traveler she had eaten for breakfast knocked against the huge logs, the fatty aroma from the remaining scraps of flesh drifting like the finest of perfumes.

Here was the question, as curious as that brat Vasilisa who had bested her by relying on the tiny magic doll she kept in her pocket. The girl who had been sent into the witch's forest to get fire and who had lived. Baba Yaga admired Vasilisa as much as she despised her.

What did a witch become when she chose to wear a costume?

Baba Yaga rocked and sipped her hot sweet tea.

What indeed? Did she dare? Would she be so bold? Yes.

She would go as what she once was—a beauty who had sold her looks for power. She would dance and sing and remember.

Yes.

And then, she would eat her fill of those pesky trick-or-treaters. There was nothing like second hand licorice taste.

"How many days until Halloween?" she asked the red horseman even though she knew the answer. It was nice to hear him say it anyway. Hear him obey her command to tell.

He bowed, his muscular body a lithe, human hook, then rose with a graceful flourish of his hands. He had thick, muscular thighs, a brush of a moustache, and dark, golden eyes. If he had a name, he knew better than to tell her. Names held power. She already held his.

"A fortnight," the red horseman told her.

Two weeks. Creeping on their own near the fire, her disembodied hands clasped bony pinkies and danced.

Three days later, Baba Yaga had finished the perfect dress, frothy midnight blue silk and periwinkle ribbon and lavender organza, lovely folds and ripples of material, perhaps a bit broader and higher in the neckline than she once used to wear. It hung perfectly on her, cosseting her every curve and line. Sure, a dress could be conjured by magic, but something in the process pulled at her. She was rarely sentimental, but *rarely* did not mean never. *This dress.* She had dreamed of this dress once upon a time. Now she had created it.

She might have finished sewing faster, but she was distracted on the first day by two lost hikers, a boy and a girl. The boy gasped, a hard choking sound, as he realized that the smooth white nobs on top of the fence posts were skulls, empty and staring. "Run," he told the girl as his eyes went wide with fear. "Run!"

But it was too late. Baba Yaga's enormous left hand was already scuttling swiftly into the yard, and even as the pair turned, it gripped tight around the girl's ankles, ripping her from the boy's grasp and sending her sprawling to her knees. The gate snapped shut, invisible locks clicking into place.

"Ohhhh," shrieked the girl. "No. Let go. Help me. Ohmygod, Harper, get it off me."

Baba Yaga stepped into the doorway, snapping the forefinger and thumb of her still-attached hand. "Come!" she said. The hand gripping the girl's tender flesh released itself.

The Bone Mother debated. She wasn't always good. Wasn't always evil. She lived a life with no moral or immoral absolutes, just pleasant, murky grey areas that made things interesting. Maybe she'd kill them. Maybe she'd let them go. Or reward them in some way, although Baba Yaga wasn't big on that particular surprise. But the trick was this: Nothing her captives would do—nothing any of them ever did—made any difference. Not prayers or deeds or supplications. Only that nettlesome Vasilisa and one other girl had ever found a way out. Since then, Baba Yaga had been much more careful.

Still. Each visitor posed a new adventure.

"Do you know how to stitch beads onto the hem of a gown?" she asked the girl. Her free hand had skipped through the dirt and was working its way up her dress and into her flapping, empty sleeve.

The boy gagged and then threw up, yellowish bile and specks of half-digested granola bar spattering his clothes. Harper. That's what the girl had called him. Clearly Harper was not cut out for such adventures.

"Do you love him?" Baba Yaga asked then. Her attention had already moved from the question of embroidery.

"I ...," said the girl. "I ... who are you? What is this?" Her voice quavered but unlike her companion, she did not lose her lunch. She struggled to her feet. Her knees were raw and bleeding.

The witch licked her lips.

"You have answered neither of my questions, dear," said Baba Yaga. She made her voice gentle and low. This always confused her captives quite deliciously. "Do you have a name, my child?"

The girl managed a glance at the boy, who was wiping his mouth with the back of his hand while tears trickled down his pasty cheeks. His eyes had gone wild and unfocused.

"I can sew," she said. "My mother taught me." She straightened her posture and held Baba Yaga's gaze. This time, the witch barely heard the tremble in her voice.

"Can you now?"

A slight nod.

The girl, nameless still, had not confessed to loving or not loving the boy. Smart, thought Baba Yaga. Clever girl. She licked her lips again. Clever girls usually tasted spicy, a fleshy mixture of cayenne and salt and the finest of smoked paprika.

"You're a witch," said the girl. "Aren't you?"

The boy was trying to run, but his feet would not move. More precisely, Baba Yaga was not letting them. He wind-milled his arms to no particular effect. In other circumstances, the motion would be comic. Actually, in *this* circumstance it was rather amusing, she had to admit.

But the girl … something vaguely maternal stirred in Baba Yaga's once shapely chest. Once, for a long while, she had kept another girl prisoner and had at times loved her like a daughter. Okay, love was stretching matters. But it had been something close to deep affection. At least now and then. She had given up the right to *actual* love, but the emotion still lingered like a ghost unable to move on.

"Come inside," she told the girl. She gestured with her long chin and smiled slowly, her iron teeth glinting in the setting sun. Baba Yaga knew she was hideous. But she knew what she had gained was worth the loss of her human good looks.

They left the boy where he was. He smelled like fear and urine, his mouth rounded in a stifled scream.

Sometimes to save yourself, you tell any lie that finds its way to your tongue. The girl—her name was Beatrice, she eventually admitted, Bea for short—had never sewn a single thing in her life, not even a button. But she attempted to embroider the lace for a number of hours, long into the night, pricking her fingers with the thin sharp needle, leaving dots of bright red blood along the hem of Baba Yaga's new gown. Sometimes, she cast a glance out the window, but once darkness came, she could no longer see the boy. At some point, a long, piercing scream followed by an odd, loud gurgle broke the quiet of the hut, and both she and witch knew there was nothing left to see.

"I wish I could let you go," Baba Yaga said with a sigh as the sun rose. Her three horsemen were saddling their mounts just outside the fence, one horse red, one black, one white. "I really do. It pains me." The girl was crying now, silent tears falling like rain.

The red horseman patted his horse, then set to arranging a new skull on a previously empty fence post.

For a moment, Baba Yaga felt pity. She took the needle from the girl's bloody fingers. "Go," she said. She made no move as the girl stumbled toward the door, making little whiffing sounds of fear. Her fingertips smeared red on the doorknob as she twisted it. Beneath them, under the floor, the chicken legs swiveled hard to the right, and the girl tripped down the steps, falling hard once again on her already bruised knees.

"Please," she whimpered. "Don't."

"Hmm," said Baba Yaga. "I said you could go." She lifted her lips in a hideous smile.

Oh why belabor the struggle? Or the spicy stew that graced the dining room table later that night? Things happen. Some of them need a little extra salt.

The following day, having finished the gown and tidily packed the leftover stew into plastic containers, Baba Yaga found just the right necklace in a shop at the town on the edge of her forest. More precisely, she found it adorning the neck of a lovely woman who had had the vast misfortune of wandering into the shop in search of antique lace. Her heart had still been beating—frantically, in fact—when Baba Yaga took the necklace from her. It had stopped not long after. Such is the consequence of having one's neck snapped along with one's pearl and ruby necklace.

"Thank you, my dear," Baba Yaga murmured as her rough hands worked the delicate clasp. She was a witch, but she was also unfailingly polite. Manners were important even when you could take whatever you wanted. She fastened the pearls and rubies around her own, thicker, neck. The baubles hung a little shorter on her, but she reveled in the smooth feel of the gems against her skin. This was a necklace of quality.

And so the rest of the fortnight passed the way fortnights do when you've got an eternal number of them at your disposal. The usual luring of small children and unwitting wanderers. The perpetual journey of her hut on its chicken legs. Things stirred and cooked in the kettle in her fireplace. Spells conjured. The occasional scrying into past and future in the skull that hovered in her fireplace. A night of festive supper and a curse for those who had attempted to outwit her. Stronger curses for those who actually had, although she had to admit a secret admiration for their moxie.

Baba Yaga was a fan of moxie.

She always had been.

A thousand years ago—this was not hyperbole; the actual number was one thousand and five plus two months—she had been a young slip of a girl. Beautiful and strong and confident and kind. And in love, because young girls are almost always in love with one thing or another. So are old women, but those stories don't always get heard because the young think that love is only for them and that they will never grow old and so they close their ears and eyes and pretend the possibility doesn't exist.

"Be careful," her mother told her, as mothers always do.

"I will," Baba Yaga said. Her name was not Baba Yaga then, of course. She had a human name and a human life and human desires and wishes and hopes and dreams.

And a man whom she secretly loved. The secrecy

made the love sweeter, of course, because that's what secrets did. Baba Yaga had absolutely no intention of being careful. Careful was for old women like her mother. Careful was for old men. Careful was no fun.

They were to meet that afternoon in the apple orchard, she and her secret lover, mid-day, when the sun was high and white in the sky and the air was filled with the scent of fruit and the sound of birds. She walked through the tall grass and imagined him. Thought of how someday soon they would be married, of the lovely gowns she would wear as his wife.

One hour. Two. He did not arrive.

She waited until the sun was setting. What if he was hurt? Surely something terrible must have happened. Why else would he not be here?

Why else indeed? She hurried back to the edge of town, pebbles jabbing the bottoms of her feet as she ran down the unpaved road in her thin-soled slippers.

"Who are you?" she said to the russet-haired girl who answered the door of her lover's cottage. She was wearing just a white cotton shift, her breasts clearly visible against the thin fabric.

Baba Yaga's lover stood behind her, lacing the leather ties at the neck of his white shirt. His black curls were a careless tangle as though someone had been stroking her fingers through them. Which, of course, someone had. "Um," he said. "We need to talk."

"No," said Baba Yaga. "I don't think we do." Something inside her hardened, and her heart pumped very, very fast. She had worried, had feared him hurt or in trouble. Betrayal had never crossed her mind. Why would it? *I love you*, he had told her night after night. *My darling. My dearest. My only.*

He followed her as she turned and walked away, easily catching up to her with his long-legged stride. She pretended not to notice as he loped beside her, and she smelled the scent of ripe apples on him, the same scent that had wafted from the other girl's long, carelessly banded hair.

"Johanne," he said, for that was Baba Yaga's human name. "I'm sorry."

She turned, and he smiled at her. His teeth were very white. His name was Wilem, and in that moment, she still loved him even as she could see now that he had never loved her. It all might have turned out differently if she had not felt that way. If she had been able to say, *Oh. I see now. Whatever was I thinking? These things happen. I will go home and eat my supper and tend to my chores*

and be glad I am free of him. Be happy that I knew be-
fore we were bound together and I was unable to leave.

But she couldn't feel any of that. Just waves of sadness and anger and humiliation. She had never expe-
rienced that last one. Not ever. It burned in her chest
like a wasp sting.

So she walked away faster this time, moving without
thinking toward the trees. "Don't follow me," she said
even though she knew he had no intention of doing so.

She wanted to hurt him. Her pain felt bright and
sharp, like a fierce diamond. Not for the loss of Wilem
exactly, although that was part of it. But for the piece of
her that believed she was above such things. That love
was easy because everything had always been easy for
her. It is hard to discover that you are just like everyone
else.

I want, she said to herself, not ready to finish the sen-
tence. *I want,* she thought again. She was in the heart of
the forest now, deeper into the woods than she had ever
ventured. She knew this was dangerous. There were
wolves and worse. Creatures. Fairies, some said. Sprites.
Unholy things. It was fully dark now. The moon was rising bright and round in the sky. But the trees were thick
and she could barely see it through the branches.

"I want," Johanne said again, this time aloud.

This time something—someone—heard her.

"You can have it all," said the woman now standing in front of her as though she had always been there in this place. She was both hideous and beautiful, her golden hair long and wild, her eyes blue as slate, her skin a deep, lustrous tawny color. "You can make him hurt as you hurt. But nothing comes without a price. Be sure, daughter."

Johanne was a smart girl. She rarely made mistakes. She rarely found herself in situations where she could make them. She was the youngest daughter. The golden girl that made them all laugh. Spoiled, even. As much as one could be spoiled in those days.

She had no idea that there were things one should never say yes to. That there were deals that could not be undone. Oh, she knew that this forest was an uncertain place. That it was dark and she was in too far and she should turn and try to find her way home.

But headstrong, beautiful girls who have been cheated on don't always think clearly.

In a fair world, everyone is entitled to one awful, furious mistake.

In the real world, sometimes one is all it takes.

"I want," Johanne said again.

"So you have said," the woman told her. "Three times plus another. So you shall have. Power. All of it. Dominion. This forest and those who abide within its boundaries. Hold out your hand, daughter."

Johanne hesitated. But she had already agreed. The woman grasped her hand tightly. Drew the tip of her dagger across the sweet flesh of Johanne's innocent, smooth palm. Three cuts. Shallow and quick.

"So you will it. So it shall be."

The transformation was as quick as the slices. The details of the bargain implied but not understood until it really was far, far too late.

She stumbled through the forest as the waves of magic slammed into her. Her bones, her skin, her veins, her blood—all of it boiled and roiled and twisted.

"Oh," she said, sounding very much like that girl who would futilely attempt to sew lace for her many years later. "Please, no."

There was no going back.

She fell to the forest floor, face buried in the dead leaves and broken twigs and bits of fur and feathers and squirmy things that crawled.

"Wilem," she cried. Then, "Mama. Papa."

No one heard her. No one came.

Twisting on the wind, she heard vague strains of tinkling laughter. "Oh daughter," said the voice. "You are such an innocent fool. But not for long."

Somewhere nearby, a wolf howled, a long, thin, startling cry.

How much time passed before she rose and lumbered to the stream a few yards away? She had no idea. All she knew was a terrible, gnawing hunger.

An apple tree sat a few feet from the water. Did apples grow in this forest? It made no sense. But she reached up and grabbed red fruit. First from the lower branches, then somehow higher, stuffing herself with juicy, tart apples. She ate and ate. Flesh and core and stem and seeds. She ate until finally, she felt she could eat no more.

Then she waded into the water, her skirts heavy but strange around her. She bent and cupped her hands and drank, gulping hard, unable to slake her thirst for many long minutes.

Finally, she lifted her head. The hunger was returning, fiercer than before. Her stomach felt like an empty pit. And what was wrong with her mouth? The stream was clear as glass as she looked down at her reflection.

"No!" she cried. "No, no, no!"

She looked away, then back. The same figure met her gaze. And the same when she inspected herself, all but her face which she could see only in watery reflection.

She was hideous.

Her face was long now and wizened, her skin like worn leather. Her nails were jagged and hard as stone. And her body—it was someone else's now: thick, her breasts pendulous, her waist and hips and legs and arms all enormous in proportion. In the water, she could see her eyes glowing black, a tiny skull in their centers instead of a pupil. Her teeth were glinting. They looked like some sort of metal—Iron?

"No," she said again, and even her voice was different now. Deep and rasping, an old, old woman's voice. A crone. A witch. A hag.

Later she would understand that beauty comes in many forms. But in this moment, all she could see was ugliness.

And Wilem. She could see him, too, standing in the center of the forest, gaping at her.

"How did you find me?" Had he really come looking? What did that mean?

His mouth opened and closed, and she watched as

he rubbed his eyes, as though he couldn't believe what he was seeing.

"It's me," she said. "Johanne."

"Witch," Wilem said. More precisely, he shrieked it. Until then, she had not taken him for a shrieker.

"Witch, witch, witch."

"How did you get here?" she asked, ignoring his babbling. The hunger in her belly was even worse now. All she wanted was to eat again. She bit her huge lower lip with her new iron teeth and tasted salty blood. It made her even hungrier.

"I don't know," he shrieked. "I was home, and now I'm here. Don't hurt me. Please don't hurt me."

Well. That wasn't quite what she hoped to hear. Although had he begged her forgiveness, it wouldn't have mattered. Either she'd kill him or she'd let him live, but that would be entirely up to her.

Unfortunately for Wilem, the hunger won.

There was a brief commotion as her right hand detached and raced toward him, leaping up and poking him in both eyes. Hard. With a squishing sound, although that was somewhat masked by his renewed shrieking. Johanne didn't find this any more or less unusual than everything else that was happening to her. It simply ... was. Her hands were removable now. Fascinating.

The end for her lover was quicker than he deserved. She was, after all, very, very hungry.

He tasted like mutton and onions and garlic and the tiniest bit of sugar.

She wiped his remains off her lips and her giant chin.

"Baba Yaga," she said, knowing without knowing how, that this was now her name.

Baba. Slavic for old woman. A negative word, but she would reclaim it. *Yaga.* A word she'd heard once from a traveling scholar. Its meanings were lost in antiquity. It meant snake maybe. Something that sneaked up on you and surprised. It would do.

Baba Yaga. Yes. This was her name.

Was still her name now as she passed the remaining days until Halloween.

She had lived many years since that day when she unwittingly traded beauty and youth for power and domination and this huge body that demanded respect above all else. The day she ceased playing by human rules. Not that humans weren't capable of huge, horrible evils. Just open the daily news feeds and there was enough callous, narcissistic behavior to make even the most ancient witch blush. But there was generally a balance. Forces that held people accountable. Rules. Laws. Social order. Body cameras. The occasional weapon of mass destruction.

But Baba Yaga had only one force. Her own.

The day of All Hallow's Eve, she collected the final pieces of her costume and flew over her forest in her giant mortar, then returned to her hut and finished the leftovers of the spicy stew she'd made from the flesh of the girl who couldn't sew.

She dressed as the sun began dipping lower in the sky. Stockings—silk and luxurious over her enormous legs. The gown, slipping over her head and falling in delicious midnight blue folds. The lovely pearl and ruby necklace that had once adorned some other woman's fragile neck.

She stood by her fireplace, the skull hovering in the flames. "I want," she said. "I want. I want."

Baba Yaga wanted many things, no different than when she had been Joanne except that now she generally got what she wanted and made sure to know what she was asking for.

She lifted her arms and covered her face with her

enormous hands. They slipped from her midnight blue sleeves and clung to her hair. In the fireplace, the skull's eyes glowed.

The transformation was swift and only slightly painful—a twinge in her bones as they grew smaller and more slender. An ache in her wrists as her hands clambered down her body and returned to their rightful place and locked tight. A swelling in her heart that she couldn't quite explain.

She knew it was just a temporary glamour. An illusion for just this night. She understood there was still no going back from what she had become so long ago. But when she peered into the fire and saw herself reflected in the skull's eyes, she still gasped with pleasure.

"Here you go, Mistress," said the horseman in blue. He held out a floral cotton pillowcase.

"Or perhaps this?" offered the horseman in black. He presented her with a tiny plastic jack-o-lantern shaped bucket.

"Or this?" suggested the horseman in red. He was holding a larger plastic bucket, this one embossed with flying, smiling bats.

Baba Yaga frowned.

"You ask for candy," the red horseman explained. "The humans give it to you if you say, 'Trick or Treat.'"

"And if I don't?" She studied the pillowcase. All the flowers were cheery daisies.

"They give you candy anyway." He held out a map of the town. One set of houses was circled in black marker.

"Are the people particularly delicious here?" she asked.

He shook his head. "They give full size candy bars. Trust me. That's a good thing."

Even powerful witches learn something new.

"Chocolate bars," said the blue horseman. "Or those ones with the peanut butter."

"Or red licorice strings," added the one in black. But Baba Yaga didn't seem to have a taste for those this evening.

In the end, it turned out she those preferred chewy, sugar-sprinkled sour candies shaped like children.

As did the little girl she compelled to walk with her so she did not look out of place. "I'm your Auntie Yaga," she instructed her. Glassy-eyed, the girl nodded. She was costumed in a beige sleeveless top, slim cut cotton trousers, and a wool hat with pom-pommed ties. Her hair was slicked back in a tidy tail.

"I'm a space warrior," the girl told her. She twirled her staff like a baton.

"Ah," Baba Yaga said. Like full-sized candy bars, this seemed a good thing.

"Your dress is beautiful," the tiny warrior told her in between bites of a fun-sized chocolate bar with almonds. "But can you fight off the Evil Empire?"

Baba Yaga considered this. The sugary chocolate aroma mixed with sweaty child was making her hungry. She nibbled on a sour candy, then popped a whole handful in her mouth and chewed blissfully.

"Absolutely," she said, mouth full.

They passed the rest of the night in companionable silence, chewing and filling their pillowcases with sweets.

Once in a while, the young warrior attempted to run, but the compelling spell held fast and the sugary treats kept her mouth occupied each time she tried to scream.

At 9 PM, the crowds of costumed revelers had thinned. A haunted house was still going strong a couple blocks over, but the rest of the neighborhood was growing quiet.

"So tell me about this Evil Empire," Baba Yaga said.

"They're a bunch of guys in capes and helmets. They

make people do things that they don't want to do."

"Well, that's nothing new," Baba Yaga said. "That's as old as time."

The girl shrugged. She readjusted her pillowcase over one slender shoulder. Her staff was dirty with mud on the bottom from where she'd dragged it as the evening had worn on.

"But not *this* space warrior," she told the witch. "She's brave and smart and tough. I think boys like her, but she doesn't care."

"Clever girl," said Baba Yaga.

"You're pretty," the girl told her then, but only because the witch compelled her to say it.

"I'm not," Baba Yaga said. She shook her head and the glamour lifted. She stood in the darkened street as her true self.

The girl's eyes went wide as saucers. She made a high-pitched, startled sound, like a mouse catching its tail in a trap.

"Run," Baba Yaga commanded her. "If you're a warrior, fight me or run."

The girl dropped her pillowcase of treats. Then she stood her ground, her chin held high, her flimsy staff held higher.

"Are you afraid of me?" Baba Yaga asked.

The girl nodded. She did not lower her staff.

They both knew it was an empty gesture. But even empty gestures can have power.

"You remind me of someone," Baba Yaga told her.

"I'm still afraid," said the girl, and something in this touched the witch's stony heart. Fear was sometimes a smart thing. Admitting it even smarter.

Baba Yaga lifted all her spells. "Oh, go on with you," she said.

The girl ran.

For now, for this one night, Baba Yaga let her go.

Joy Preble is the author of several young adult novels including the *Dreaming Anastatia* series; the *Sweet Dead Life* series; and *Finding Paris*, which *SLJ* called, "An intricate guessing game of sisterly devotion, romance, and quiet desperation." Her newest novel, *It Wasn't Always Like This*, was called "epic and addictive" by *Beautiful Creatures'* author Kami Garcia and "a suspenseful treat with a gooey romantic center" by the *Bulletin of the Center for Children's*

Books. In no particular order, Joy is fond of her family, her basset-boxer, clever cocktails, crazy road trips, and people who don't whine. She's also the Children's Specialist at Houston's Brazos Bookstore and on faculty at Writespace Houston. Visit Joy at joypreble.com or follow her at @joypreble on Twitter.

Some Like It Hot
Mari Mancusi

No doubt about it, thought Ashlee Firebreath as she pushed open the door and scrambled down the front steps of what was once, five minutes, thirty three second ago, Stanley Rosenblum's family's ancestral home. *I am destined to be the last girl to be kissed at Brackenridge High.*

From the sidewalk she glanced back at the house. Or what was left of it, anyway—its second story now completely engulfed by flames. The thick smoke clouded her view and filled her lungs, causing her to hold back a choke. Not that her lungs couldn't take a little soot, but still. She was more used to exhaling it than breathing it in.

Stanley Rosenblum stood a few feet away, also staring up at the raging inferno, a look of ultimate dismay on his admittedly pig-like face. She'd made sure he gotten out first, of course. That he didn't burn any essential body parts or pass out on the stairs from inhaling too much smoke. Sometimes that happened, forcing her to fly them out to safety.

From the look on Stanley Rosenblum's face now she could tell he'd rather die than let her fly him anywhere. So it was fortunate for him he had good lung capacity.

"You!" he cried, turning to face her now. He shook his fist at her, his chubby, freckled cheeks burning red with rage. "You're a monster!"

Hm. She studied him skeptically as the fire engines wailed ever closer. He certainly hadn't thought that five minutes thirty four seconds earlier. When they were on the couch, pretending to watch Netflix as he slobbered on her neck like a St. Bernard who had just discovered a raw rib eye ripe for the taking.

Bleh.

To be fair, Stanley Rosenblum wouldn't have been her first choice for her first kiss. In fact, he pretty much bottomed out a really, really, *really* long list. But he had been there, he had been willing, and she had been desperate.

Not to mention it was rumored at school that Stanley's mom had once been married to a were-salamander and that Stanley was the progeny of that unholy union. And weren't salamanders supposed to be fireproof or something?

She sighed. Well, Stanley might have been. But his house clearly wasn't.

The screeching wail of Ladder 45 was getting closer and she knew she had to vacate the premises ASAP—before she was forced to face some awkward questioning from the authorities. Walking over to Stanley, she grabbed him by the shoulders and caught his angry hazel eyes with her own deep golden ones.

"You will remember nothing!" she told him. "*Nothing!*"

She let him go. Then she waited. Right on cue, Stanley's eyes went blank. His mouth went slack. His hands dropped to his side. She nodded grimly. It was always slightly disconcerting to realize how easily human eyes could lose focus and glaze over. But it was certainly necessary, given the circumstances.

She poked him a few more times, to make sure he'd achieved the necessary catatonic state she needed for survival, then took off down the road, praying the fire department might arrive in time to find something salvageable.

Ugh. She had to stop doing this. The local news reporters had already declared there was a serial arsonist loose in town. *The Brackenridge Burner*, they'd dubbed her. Four houses in three months. All damaged by mysterious fires that broke out at odd times (though almost always after school or on weekends). Each time a resident of the house in question—always a high school boy, usually good looking but sometimes less so—was found outside the home. But each time that hot (or not so hot) boy just drooled and pointed at his former residence, remembering nothing of how it had been torched.

And each time, Ashlee Firebreath remained unkissed.

Turning the corner, past the old Opera House, she entered a small park at the center of town. There, she leaned over, front claws on her back haunches, attempting to catch her breath and stop the burn. A moment later she felt her talons receding into her fingers and the scales on her chest melting back into her skin. Her ears shrank back to normal person size and her nose back to normal Ashlee size (which was admittedly a bit larger than your average person's, but save a nose job, what could she do?)

She looked down into the fountain, sighing in relief as her reflection stared back up at her. The reflection of a normal eighteen-year-old girl. Blond hair, blue eyes, a cute figure. The kind of girl any boy would have loved to make out with. If only she could manage to control herself long enough to allow him to do it.

Seriously, sometimes being a were-dragon was a tough break.

Because, you see, ever since Ashlee had hit puberty when she became hot, she became very hot. Which caused an instant shift into dragon form—and often a burp of fire to boot. Which, as you might imagine, could cause quite a problem when it came to making out with cute boys. And thus, at practically the old maid age of eighteen years old, she still had not managed to achieve that perfect first kiss.

It wasn't for lack of trying, either. Her first attempt had been in the back of Lester Birnbaum's mother's ancient station wagon. You know the type, the kind with wood paneling on the side that they haven't made in like fifty years? Well, turned out the wood was fake. But the vinyl seats still melted alarmingly quickly when you applied a little heat. Lester—a total Ryan Reynolds lookalike she'd been dreaming about for weeks—only had to touch her shoulder when she first felt it. A change deep inside of her. A growing heat that threatened to consume her. She stumbled out of the car, luckily before the shift was complete (or else she might still be stuck inside to this day!), then opened her mouth to release the pressure building inside like a volcano.

To be fair, she tried to turn her head away. But at the last minute Lester, understandably terrified, had stumbled out after her and had inadvertently jumped right into her path, just as the flames shot from her mouth. They ignited his hair, his mother's station wagon, and a few trees nearby. (Though technically speaking those trees were on their last legs anyway, so it wasn't truly fair to count them as part of the destruction tally, in Ashlee's opinion.)

"It's not me, it's you," Lester informed her a few minutes later, breaking up with her as they waited for the fire department to arrive, clearly more than a little annoyed by the fact that he now looked more like *Deadpool* Ryan Reynolds versus, say *Green Lantern.*

To be honest, she couldn't really blame him. And unfortunately back then she didn't even know how to hypnotize guys into forgetting the unfortunate events that had transpired between them. And the next day at school Lester told everyone who was anyone about her little smoky snafu, which sadly led to some very lonely Friday nights for Ashlee sophomore year.

Junior year wasn't much better. That was the year of the exploding chem lab that had sent her home with a week's suspension. Which was completely unfair, by the way, seeing as Federal regulations clearly state that all flammable chemicals should be stored in flameproof cases. Which had led her to the very logical assumption that sneaking into the chem lab closet to make out with Buster Brim would be perfectly safe. After all, how was she to know Gary Gorisnky, in a hurry to get to football practice after class, had forgotten to put away all those pesky bottles of nitroglycerin?

And so it continued. Guy after guy, near kiss after near kiss, the pattern as endless as it was predictable. They'd hold her hand. She'd spout flames. They'd go running in the other direction. She'd go get a snow cone to cool off. Depressing, really.

It was her parents' fault, in case you were wondering. Her adopted father, St. George, had shown up just a tad too late to save her virgin mother—whose village had decided to sacrifice her to a local were-dragon to keep the peace. St. George, who always had a crush on her mom, went all knight in shining armor on the place, determined to go and rescue his true love.

What he didn't realize was she and the were-dragon had been getting on like a house on fire (so to speak) and would have been quite content to play happily ever after in the dragon's den for all of all of eternity. (Which was warm and safe and filled with enough gold to buy out an entire shoe store!) Unfortunately George—having the best of intentions, but not a ton of smarts—hacked her new boyfriend in two without bothering to ask if that was cool or not. Before she could protest—the damage was done. The dragon was dead.

George, feeling more than a little guilty (not to mention embarrassed) by the incident had tried to make the best of things by asking her mother for her hand in marriage. She somewhat grudgingly accepted (her only other option being to go back to the village who sold her out to a dragon in the first place) and nine months later a little were-dragon named Ashlee Firebreath (after her dear old dad) was born.

Ashlee loved both her parents and honestly had had a very pleasant upbringing overall, here in Brackenridge Falls—a place where thankfully you didn't have to be human to fit in. There were witches here and vampires and werewolves and countless other creatures all making their homes in the town. There were even a growing number of were-armadillos on the east side who had recently opened a Medieval Times. While in other places being a were-dragon would cause you to stick out like a sore claw, here she barely registered on the weird scale.

Still, that didn't make the kissing thing any easier.

Sighing, she turned the corner and walked down her street, headed home. When she got to her front door, her mother was standing there, arms crossed over her chest and a disapproving look on her face. Uh, oh.

"Ashlee Firebreath," she said in a tight voice. The one she reserved for when her daughter was in big trouble. "Why do I hear fire engines and smell smoke?"

"Uh, because there's a fire somewhere and our brave Brackenridge firefighters are valiantly dousing the blaze?" Ashlee tried in her most innocent voice. Too bad her mind control tricks didn't work on family.

"And who might be responsible for that fire, may I ask?" Her mother raised an eyebrow, peering at her with suspicious eyes.

"It's really not that big of a deal, Mom," Ashlee protested, realizing she was busted. "It's just a teeny, tiny thing, really. They'll be able to put it out easily. Why, I bet it didn't even cause any real damage."

To the first floor, anyway. Maybe ...

"You've been dating boys again, haven't you?" her mother scolded. "What have I told you about that?"

"I'm eighteen years old, Mom!" Ashlee cried. Seriously, sometimes it sucked to have an ex-professional virgin as a mother. "Everyone else at school has been dating for like three years now."

"Everyone else is not half-dragon," her mother reminded her. "I've told you a thousand times. When you reach the age of dragon maturity, we'll be happy to find you a suitable beau."

"That's almost a thousand years away, Mom! I can't stay a virgin for another millennium."

"There's nothing wrong with being a virgin," huffed her mother.

"Oh yeah, it worked out real great for you. Your village sacrificed you to a freaking dragon."

"Obviously no one does that in this day and age, Ash," her mother said. "You know that. And besides, it was a great … honor to be selected as a sacrifice to Drake," she added.

Even under the dim glow of the street lamps, Ashlee noticed her mother's cheeks flush as she voiced her dad's name aloud. As much as Mom professed to loving St. George, the woman never failed to blush and stammer when someone brought up Drake. Guess even professional virgins could have a thing for bad boys ….

Ashlee looked down at her phone. "Mom, I gotta grab my bag and go. I'm late to meet Sarah at the library.

We're supposed to work on our history project."

Her mother reluctantly stepped aside, allowing Ashlee to enter the house and grab her school bag. While she didn't approve of Ashlee having a boyfriend, she thankfully had no issue with her hanging with her best friend Sarah. Sarah was apprenticing as a demon slayer while taking part time classes at Brackenridge High. The two girls had first bonded over a shared love for *Supernatural* (Sarah was a Dean Girl while Ashlee had always swooned over Sam) and the rest was history.

Until recently, when Sarah had gone and rubbed an old lamp at an antique swap. (She claimed it was just to see if it was real silver, but Ashlee didn't buy that for one second.) In any case, a moment later a totally hot genie named Trevor had popped out and instantly professed himself Sarah's love slave for all eternity. Which, in Ashlee's opinion, was so not fair. Especially since Sarah claimed she wasn't even interested in the guy, yet he followed her around like a lovesick puppy everywhere she went.

While Ashlee walked around with the dragon equivalent of boy-repellent.

She headed out the door. "Bye, Mom," she called, swinging her bag over her shoulder.

"Bye sweetie," Her mom cried back, waving. "Have fun. And remember—no boys!"

Groan. "Yes, mom."

Shaking her head—*Mothers!*—Ashlee headed down to the public library where she found Sarah sitting in a corner table, dressed in her usual hipster homeless apparel that somehow didn't manage to detract from her supermodel good looks. Even her ridiculous t-shirt ("I'm a Slayer, Ask Me How!") looked good on her and made Ashlee suddenly realize she should have glanced in a mirror or at least run a brush through her own hair before meeting up with her friend. After all, a dragon shift, not to mention a five-alarm fire and an almost kiss, could leave a girl looking a little less fresh and fabulous than normal.

Sarah caught her eye and waved her over. The two girls exchanged hugs then sat across from one another, pulling out their homework.

"So how's Trevor?" Ashlee teased, knowing the devoted genie was a sore spot for her friend.

Sarah rolled her eyes. "I'm trying to forget he exists, thank you very much."

"At least you have a love slave. I can't even get someone to kiss me." Ashlee quickly gave her friend the rundown on what had had happened with Stanley.

"Wow. That's rough, Ash," Sarah said when she'd finished. "Seriously, I'd never guess someone like Stanley Rosenblum was capable of getting you hot enough to spout flames. After all, he's not exactly Chris Hemsworth."

"He's not even Chris Christie," Ashlee agreed miserably. "Clearly I'm so repressed that even a freaking were-gerbil would turn me on if he stuck his buck teeth out in my direction."

"There's got to be someone who can take your heat ...." Sarah tapped her fingers on her textbook as she thought. Then she closed her eyes and groaned. "Oh man."

"What?"

"You are so going to owe me for this one," she grumbled.

"What, already?"

"I could ask Trevor. I mean, if you really wanted me to. I hate asking him for anything. He's already too darn arrogant for his own good. But if it would help you out ...."

"Really? You'd do that?"

Sarah sighed, evidently resigned. "Sure, why not?

He's a genie, right? He has to know tons of guys in low places." She let out a sharp whistle. "Hey Trevor! I know you're lurking nearby and listening in on our private conversation. You might as well show yourself." She rolled her eyes at Ashlee. "Seriously, the dude's worse than Edward Cullen at a sleepover. I've half a mind to—"

Before she could finish Trevor had appeared—out of thin air? Ashlee couldn't quite tell. But she had to admit, stalker-like or not, it was hella convenient. Instant Love Slave! Just add water!

"I believe I'd like some of those pancake foods again, oh lovely goddess of all that is good and righteous and holy and amazing," Trevor said smoothly, taking a seat across from the girls as if this was all just Tuesday in his everyday supernatural existence.

Ashlee tried her best not to stare at him. But holy crap, he was hot. Like the guy from the new Superman movie hot. Jet black hair, piercing silver eyes. Cheekbones that looked as if they were cut from glass. Seriously, Sarah was so lucky, and she didn't even seem to realize it.

Instead, she was giving the genie a disproving look. "It's *pancakes*," she stated flatly. "Not pancake foods, not round discs of syrupy awesome. Just pancakes." She sounded irritated. "And we can eat later. First we've got important business to discuss. Namely my friend Ash here. She's in desperate need of a boyfriend."

"*Not* a boyfriend," Ashlee piped in. "At this point I'm just looking to get kissed."

"You shouldn't have any trouble with that," Trevor remarked, giving Ash a quick once over with those intense, burning eyes of his. A look so hot that Ashlee had to fight back the urge to shift right then and there. After all, the last thing she wanted was for her friend to think she had some kind of attraction to her new guy. Sarah may have found Trevor annoying as anything, but she was oddly possessive of him at the same time.

Sure enough, her friend snapped her fingers. "Watch it," she growled at Trevor. "You're *my* professed love slave for all eternity, remember? Last I checked I've still got plenty of time on that clock."

"Of course, lovely mortal goddess of amazing power and beauty and wits," Trevor purred putting an arm around her shoulder. She shoved him off, but not before Ashlee caught a secretly pleased look scamper across her face.

"Anyway, you know any guys you can hook her up

with?" she asked. "Someone who can ... take a little heat? She's part dragon, you know. So we're looking for a friend who's fireproof."

Trevor thought for a moment, then his odd silver eyes lit up. "Maybe my friend Julian?" he suggested. "Nice fire demon. Resides in Hell's Kitchen." He glanced at Ashlee consideringly. "That's not going to be a problem is it?"

"Hell's Kitchen in New York City? Actually I hear that's a pretty up and coming neighborhood."

"Uh, no. Hell's Kitchen in, well, Hell," Trevor corrected, looking a little sheepish. "Julian's dad is Satan's sous chef."

Ashlee raised an eyebrow. "Satan's sous chef? Are you serious?"

"Of course. Dude makes a mean flambé. And because he's a demon his skin is completely flame retardant." He looked pleased with himself.

"Uh, right. But Hell? Like, actual Hell?" Ashlee sputtered. "Like fire and brimstone and all that jazz? I mean, isn't the place unbearably hot to begin with?"

"It's a dry heat," Trevor explained, looking a little offended.

"Uh, hello?" Sarah interrupted, waving two hands

in Ashlee's face. "The guy's male. He likes to play with fire. And he can cook. Since when did you get all picky?" Her friend huffed. "You just tried to get it on with Stanley Rosenbaum for goodness's sake."

"Please don't remind me," Ashlee groaned, feeling her face heat. "But you're right. Julian sounds great. And hey, this is just for a quick kiss, right? It's not like I'm committing to marriage here or even looking for a boyfriend ...." She paused then added. "So ... when can I meet him?"

So that's how, three days later, Ashley Firebreath, were-dragon from Brackenridge Falls came to be knocking on Julian the Fire Demon from Hell's front door. She'd dressed for the occasion, in a lacy, sleeveless dress that fit both the weather (dry heat—whatever) and her mission (looking super cute could only help her cause, right?) Still, by the time she knocked, she was sweating a bit, and not only because of the heat.

What would Julian be like? Would he be cute? Nice? Most importantly—kissable?

Then the door swung open, and Ashlee's mouth followed along with it, her jaw practically dropping to the floor. At first she legit wondered if she might have the wrong house. After all, the boy who poked his head outside looked absolutely nothing like what she'd pictured. Mostly because while Trevor had assured her his friend was hot, she'd imagined it'd be in some big, bulky Vin Diesel jock-type way. Flaming red skin, pointy horns, a little goatee perhaps. You know, fire demon chic.

But this guy! He was like the complete opposite. Tall, slender, with thick, wavy hair the color of wheat. And his eyes! Vivid, green, almost glowing with their intensity. This guy was a fire demon? If she'd met him on the streets she would have assumed him an angel instead.

"You must be Ashlee," he said, his luscious mouth curving into a friendly smile, revealing perfect white teeth. She drew in a breath. God, he was cute. Wait— not God. Was it bad manners to use the word God when on a date in Hell?

She really should have Googled all this beforehand.

"Yes, hi," she stammered, hoping she didn't look as flushed as she felt as she held out her hand. Hopefully this guy really could take some heat, as Trevor had promised. Because she was starting to smolder just by looking at him. "I'm Ashlee. Nice to meet you!"

He reached out, closing his large hand over hers. A casual shake—that literally left her shaking. And as she followed him inside, she forced herself to take in an (also shaky) breath.

Don't wimp out now, she scolded herself. *Not when you're so close to finally getting what you want.*

Because, she realized, she was about to get kissed. For the very first time in her life. And, this time, there was nothing to stop it from happening.

She wondered if it would come naturally. Or if it'd be awkward at first—like they'd bump noses or something. Her nose was, as previously mentioned, a little large to begin with. But it got practically snout-like when she shape-shifted into a dragon. Hopefully that wouldn't be a problem for her date.

"Would you like a soda or water or something?" Julian asked, breaking into her crazy thoughts.

"Water would be great," she said. After all, her nerves were already as taut as piano wire. No need to add caffeine to the mix.

Julian nodded, heading into the kitchen. He returned a moment later with two large mason jars. "Hope you don't mind room temperature," he apologized. "We don't have a lot of refrigeration down here."

"Really?" she asked, taking the cup from him. "So you don't eat anything cold? How do you keep food from spoiling?"

"Amazon Pantry."

"Excuse me?" She raised an eyebrow.

"It's changed everything," Julian said excitedly. "Now we can get pretty much anything we want, delivered overnight, right to our front doors. And some places do have refrigeration," he amended. "Like the Starbucks on Brimstone Ave. They just got a Frapaccino machine. You should have seen the line in the morning."

Ashlee didn't know whether to be impressed or horrified that Starbucks had opened up a store in hell. Evidently the coffee chain really was taking over the world—er, or underworld, as the case might be.

"So," she said nervously, glancing around the house again, wondering how they could segue into the kissing. Should she just walk up to him and press her lips against his, see how it went? Or did they need to talk it over first, let it come naturally?

"So," he repeated. He walked over to the far side of the room, staring at the bookshelf there, as if he held all the secrets to the universe. She raised an eyebrow.

Was he being shy? This big, bad demon from hell? Or... she frowned. Had he changed his mind? Maybe he didn't find her attractive, now that they were face to face. Which would be just her luck, right? Finally she'd found a flameproof guy, only to learn he was just not that into her.

"Are you hungry?" he asked suddenly. "I cooked some dinner."

Ashlee startled, realizing for the first time that the adjoining dining room had been all set up for a fancy meal. White linen tablecloth, candles, silver service for two. Wow. He'd obviously gone through a lot of trouble for her.

Something inside her stomach squirmed. She wondered if she should tell him she didn't need this level of seduction. Kissing him was the whole point of coming here—there was no need to butter her up.

"I'm not really hungry," she started to say, only to have her stomach betray her with a loud groan. Her cheeks flushed bright red. She hadn't eaten lunch today, being too nervous about the whole meeting a stranger in Hell thing. And now, evidently, her body was launching a protest.

"Sure," she amended. "I'd love to eat."

"Great!" Julian looked relieved. She watched as he walked over to the dining room table and pulled out a chair for her. A gesture, she couldn't help but note, none of her previous dates had bothered to try to do. Not to mention no one had ever thought to cook for her before!

And so, against her better judgment, she went over and sat down. Julian smiled and disappeared into the kitchen, returning a moment later with a delicious smelling roast. He set it down on the table then proceeded to bring out the side dishes. Mountains of mashed potatoes, carrots and green beans. Puffy white rolls. She hadn't sat at a feast like this in ages.

She took a tentative bite. "Delicious!" she exclaimed, surprised. For some reason she had assumed all food down here would taste a little burnt. But this— this was making her taste buds do a happy dance in her mouth. Maybe she needed to lay off stereotyping this place. Not to mention Julian himself.

"Thanks," he said, his ears reddening a bit in the most adorable way. "My dad taught me how to cook."

She nodded. Right. His Dad. Satan's sous chef. This whole night was becoming more surreal by the second.

Julian took a bite of food. "So tell me about yourself,"

he said after chewing and swallowing. "What's it like being a were-dragon?" He smiled. "I'm guessing it's way cooler than being an ex-angel."

She snorted. "I don't know about that."

"Really?"

"Let's just say being a shape shifter in suburbia comes with its own set of complications."

And then, to her surprise, she started telling him about those complications. Which she totally hadn't meant to do. After all, this was supposed to be just about kissing. Not confessing one's life story to a complete stranger.

And yet here she was, telling him about her mom. About her stepdad killing her father to rescue her mom. She told him about the unfortunate incident in the chem lab sophomore year. And about being nicknamed Fire Freak by the other kids after the unfortunate car conflagration with Lester Birnbaum—and how it had taken an entire year of amensia'ing her fellow classmates to finally get them to lay off.

It was pretty pathetic, as far as life stories went. But Julian listened attentively. He asked questions at the right times. And when she had finished, instead of running shrieking in the other direction, he looked at her with something that weirdly seemed to resemble admiration. Which was crazy, of course. And also sent an unexpected warmth rising from her stomach that had nothing to do with the delicious food.

"What about you?" she asked, pushing the warmth back down. After all, shifting into a dragon before dessert would be more than a little awkward, not to mention totally bad manners. "How'd you end up down here? And how did your dad become Satan's chef? I mean, that seems like a pretty big deal, no?"

'It is," Julian agreed. "But then he's the only guy in a hundred mile radius who can make a decent angel's food cake."

She raised an eyebrow. He laughed.

"Yeah, I know. It's weird, right? But the big boss has an unquenchable hunger for the stuff. Angel food addict, some might say." He winked at her. "But don't tell anyone I told you. Would totally ruin his rep."

"So ... you guys used to be angels then?" she asked, remembering the story of how some angels were cast out of Heaven. Perhaps this family was one of them.

Julian sighed. "Yes. I was born in Heaven. Grew up with the wings, the halo, the works. Until my dad got his new gig and moved us down here. Said it would be an adventure." He wrinkled his nose to tell her exactly what he thought about *that*.

Ashlee couldn't help but laugh. "So, I take it Hell isn't exactly a hot spot then?"

He groaned. "I'm sure it's fine if you grew up here. But all my friends and family are still up above. Down here, I don't know a soul. Well, not that anyone has a soul here," he amended. "You pretty much have to check them in on arrival. But all the other demons have known each other since kindergarten and aren't really interested in becoming friends with a weird looking ex-angel like me."

Ashlee felt her heart wrench a little as she took in the sad look on his face. He was lonely, she realized with surprise. The big, bad fire demon from Hell was actually lonely. Suddenly she felt a pinch of guilt. Here she was, down here with the sole intention of borrowing his flameproof lips to mark something off her bucket list. While he was clearly looking for something much more.

But no. He was a guy, right? And guys were always cool with kissing. Especially kissing with no strings attached. Besides, it wasn't as if Trevor hadn't told him the deal when setting up the date. He knew what this was. All it could turn out to be.

She pushed away from her chair. She needed to get this show on the road before she lost her nerve. "That was delicious," she declared. "Now about that ..."

She trailed off. He looked up at her, expectantly. She frowned. Tried to push the word "kiss" from her lips. But somehow it seemed stuck in her throat. Her knees buckled a little, her heart hammering her chest. Oh, dear.

Was she going to blow this all over again?

Julian rose to his feet. She took an involuntary step backward, not able to help but notice again how good-looking he was. How tall he was. How broad his shoulders were. How his eyes seemed to glow in the dim light. He took a step toward her. Her breath caught in her throat. Was this it? Was this what she'd been waiting for all night? What she'd been waiting for her entire life?

Do not chicken out. Do not chicken out.

He stopped. "Would you like to go for a flight?"

Wait, what?

She stared at him, for a moment speechless. Then she finally found her voice. "Flight?" she stammered.

A slow smile stretched across his face. "Usually after

a big meal I like to get out. Stretch my wings."

"But you don't have any—"

"Invisible."

"What?"

"My wings are invisible until I'm ready to use them."

"Dude, that's so cool!" she blurted out, before she could stop herself.

He shrugged, but looked pleased by her assessment. "So what do you say? Want to take a quick flight?"

"I don't know …." She shuffled from foot to foot, suddenly a little embarrassed. After all, he was a hot ex-angel with invisible wings. She was a weird dragon with horns and a tail. What was he going to think of her after seeing her shifted? What if he was totally turned off? What if he decided she was not kissable after all?

"Come on," he said. "You're not scared of flying through Hell, are you?"

She frowned, a little offended. "Of course not."

"Then what you waiting for?"

She sighed. "Okay, okay. Let's do it."

A quick flight. A quick romantic flight to get them both in the mood. No big deal.

And so she followed him outside. Watched him unfurl his wings. She let out a low whistle as the golden feathers caught the light—so brilliant they were almost blinding. Not to mention he had some serious wing-span going on. Which only made him hotter.

And only made her feel even more insecure.

He turned, looking at her expectantly. For a moment she considered running away, right then and there. Never looking back. Then she sighed and closed her eyes, concentrating on making the shift. After all, what was the worst that could happen? He'd think her weird. Ugly. They wouldn't kiss. And she would be right back where she started, no big deal.

The first shimmer of change began to shiver over her, silver scales sprouting from her skin. A moment later she felt her nose elongating. Then wings, popping out from her shoulder blades. She dropped to all fours, her hands transforming into feet, fingernails curling into claws.

People always asked if it hurt to shift, but actually it was just the opposite. It felt good. Like taking off a costume after a long Halloween night. Which was odd and the opposite of what it should have felt like, but there you go.

When the transformation was complete, she turned to Julian, surprised to see him looking at her with clear awe in his eyes. She made a face, feeling sheepish. Thankfully dragons couldn't blush. "I know I look weird," she stammered.

"If by weird you mean completely bad ass," he replied, without missing a beat. He grinned. "I am so jealous right now, I can't even tell you."

"Yeah, yeah," she muttered, wondering if he was just trying to be nice. But no, he looked completely sincere. And suddenly a weird feeling of pride started to flutter deep within her. Which was crazy, of course. She couldn't remember the last time she felt proud of her dragon self—if ever. She thought back to all those loser kids at school. If only they could see her now. Side by side with the coolest ex-angel in Hell.

Julian smiled at her. "Are you ready?" he asked.

She nodded, feeling her own smile flash across her scaly face. "Let's do this."

And so they did. Spreading their wings, taking to the skies. And soon Ashlee found herself enjoying that delicious feeling of the wind whipping at her face as her wings found the air currents, riding them like a wave. Julian kept up easily, flying by her side and though they must have looked like a very unlikely pair, she soon began to have too much fun to care.

She didn't fly very much at home—it would be too embarrassing if she were seen by any of her friends. But here she didn't know a soul. (Er, non-soul.) Here she could just enjoy the ride.

Not to mention the company. As they flew, they chatted with one another. The conversations ranging from gas guzzling SUVs (the guy who invented them was now evidently peddling a bike around the ninth circle of hell) to a lively debate on whether Heaven would be a red or blue state. They even shared a laugh over the fetching antics of Satan's dog Cerberus. (The woofer had apparently gotten excruciatingly fat, having the ability to beg for scraps from three different tables at once.)

In all, Ashlee couldn't remember having such a fun evening. And soon she'd pretty much forgotten all about her mission to kiss.

That was, until they finally settled back to the ground, in front of Julian's house. He folded his wings and she forced herself back to human shape. He smiled at her. "That was fun," he said. "I can't remember the last time I had anyone to fly with."

She nodded. "Same here. Back home we have a few fairies who can fly. But they're total snobs. If I fly, it's always just been me."

"Well, not anymore," he declared. "Anytime you want to stretch your wings, just text me."

"Awesome," she said. And she meant it, too. Then she glanced at her watch. "Oh! It's late. I had no idea!" She'd been having so much fun she totally missed curfew. Her mom was going to kill her.

"Sorry," Julian said. "I didn't notice the time. Do you want me to call you an Uber to cross the River Styx?"

"That'd be great actually." She rose to her feet, feeling suddenly awkward. Julian busied himself with the Uber app on his phone. Then he looked up.

"All set. He should be here in five minutes."

It was then that she remembered her mission again. Her whole point for being here in the first place. After the whole dinner and flying and great conversation she'd almost forgotten. But now—she had five minutes to get the job done. To score that first kiss—once and for all. Her heart pounded in her chest. She could not blow this again, not after all the trouble she'd gone through to get here. If nothing else, Sarah would never let her hear the end of it!

And so, drawing in a breath, she took a step forward toward Julian. He raised an eyebrow, giving her a look that she decided was cautiously interested as she took another step forward, her heart hammering in her chest. Their faces were now inches apart, and she captured his eyes with her own, as if daring him to turn away.

He didn't.

"Hi," she whispered.

"Um, hi," he whispered back, a small smile playing on his lips. He reached out, running his hand through her blond hair, his fingers lightly scraping her scalp. It felt so nice she almost purred with pleasure. And the heat inside of her began to build in the most pleasant way.

But just as she was about to close her eyes, tilt her head, get this over with once and for all, Julian took a quick step backward. Out of her arms. Out of her reach.

The effect was like jumping into a cold shower. "What's wrong?" she demanded, hating how desperate her voice sounded. *Play it cool,* she scolded herself.

He shrugged, his face reddening a bit. "Nothing," he assured her. "I just think ... well, maybe we should slow things down a bit."

She squinted her eyes at him. "Slow down?" she

repeated, confused and concerned. "But ..."

He gave her a rueful look. "I'm sorry, okay? I know why you came here. And believe me, I was totally willing to help you out. Before I met you, that is."

Ouch. Disappointment dropped to her stomach like a rock. And here she thought the night had been going so well, That they'd had such a great time. Made a real connection even. Had it all been only her imagination?

"Don't you ...?" She struggled for the words. "Want me?" she spit out at last, feeling stupid and hot. And not in the 'turned on' kind of way this time.

To her surprise. Julian started to laugh.

A scowl crossed her face. "What's so funny?" she demanded, now feeling a little sick to her stomach to boot. Was the idea of him wanting her *that* ridiculous?

"Sorry," Julian said, shaking his head and giving her an apologetic look. "It's just ... are you kidding me? I can't imagine any red-blooded angel or demon not wanting someone like you."

"Then why are you rejecting me?" she demanded, finding it hard to speak past the lump in her throat. *Don't cry!* she scolded herself. *Whatever you do, don't let him see you cry.*

"Wait—is that what you think?" He looked surprised.

When she shrugged he took a step forward, reaching out to place his hands on her arms. Then he met her eyes with his own.

"I assure you, Ashlee Firebreath" he said in a low voice. "I am not rejecting you. Not even close." He paused, his eyes twinkling. "But I'm not going to kiss you. Not tonight anyway."

"Why?" She could barely breathe at this point.

"Because then it'd be all over," he said simply. "You'd get your kiss. And while I'm sure I'd enjoy the hell out of that kiss—no pun intended." He grinned wickedly. "What I want from you is so much more."

She stared at him, hardly able to breathe. Definitely unable to speak. The way he was looking at her now—with such affection in his eyes—it was hard to even describe it.

He reached out again, this time slipping his hand into hers. His fingers moving across her skin, sending shivers down to her toes. Then he gave her a cautious smile. "Ashley, you're smart. You're funny. You're amazing. You're the first girl I've met in this god-forsaken place who could make me forget we were thrown out of Heaven." He squeezed her hand in his.

It was then that she felt it. Not the cheap, raging

fire she normally felt rise within her at a boy's touch. The kind that made her want to explode and shift and spout flame. But rather a slow burn. A tender warmth.

And suddenly she understood. Being kissed wasn't the important thing here. It was just a technicality that would someday take care of itself. Here, in the strangest place, with the most unexpected guy, she'd found something better. Something she hadn't even realized she was searching for.

Ashlee Firebreath, were-dragon of Brackinridge Falls had not just found a guy who could take her heat. She'd found a guy who could keep her warm.

She looked up at Julian. All earlier self-consciousness fading away. Then she smiled. "Fair enough," she said. "But someday soon I'm going to get you to give me that first kiss."

He grinned back at her. "I'll hold you to that."

And, at that moment, she knew, without a doubt, that he would

And that it would be so worth the wait.

Mari Mancusi always wanted a dragon as a pet. Unfortunately the fire insurance premiums proved a bit too large and her house a bit too small—so she chose to write about them instead. Today she works as an award-winning young adult author and freelance television producer, for which she has won two Emmys. When not writing about fanciful creatures of myth and legend, Mari enjoys traveling, cosplay, anything Disney, watching cheesy (and scary) horror movies, and her favorite guilty pleasure—playing videogames. A graduate of Boston University, she lives in Austin, Texas, with her husband Jacob, daughter Avalon, and their two dogs.

The Fragrant Feast
Sarah Lyn Eaton

Evening birds trilled their last songs as Louise walked through the woods, struggling with the heavy basket in her arms. It wasn't her first time carrying the feasting supplies across the yard, but she had never done it wearing an antique Civil War era gown. *How did women wear these every day?*

Young Louise took her time, fearful with every step that she'd trip on the hem hidden beneath her heavy bundle. She was grateful that the long skirts hid her trusty Vans. The old woman had said the dress was important. Even the old-fashioned curls in her hair had been necessary, but she'd said nothing about shoes.

Odie had said it was time. The stars had told her so. And Louise prepared as she was instructed, carrying the necessary ingredients through the old oak grove.

Copal smoke sweetly thickened the night air as Louise reached a break in the trees. In a private cemetery, the old woman walked among the tombstones, some of them so old the inscribed words were illegible. Wrinkled hands struck match after match, lighting candles as beacons. The old woman stopped at a last tombstone, where metal-framed photos had been set around the base. Louise watched the elder light the final rose-scented candles, nestled in a peppery marigold wreath. The candle flames flickered in the growing greylight.

Louise took a deep breath at the entrance. She was the youngest ever to be called to host the family feast, but she was ready. When she stepped through the gate, she stepped into the part she had trained to play. *This year,* she prayed, *everything changes.*

"Odie," Louise dropped the heavy picnic basket on an empty table. "I have the pan de muerto."

"You made it as instructed?" The old woman's voice challenged.

"I followed your recipe to the letter," Louise assured her, "though it was not the same as making it with you."

"It takes me longer every year to set up this feast," Odie exhaled sharply. Her bones cracked as she righted herself and stretched. "Besides, it'll be your kitchen soon enough." The woman named Ordelia turned. Her jaw unhinged softly. "Ghosts alive!"

"Do I look all right?" Louise kept the skirt low and gave a slow twirl.

"Beautiful." Tears glistened in Ordelia's eyes. She touched her heart. "You almost sent me into my next life. Like you stepped out of another era."

Louise closed her eyes. She knew the old woman was seeing into another time. Odie was old enough to have known the original owner of the dress she wore. Louise scowled.

"That face won't do," the woman frowned.

"Then stop talking about dying," Louise countered.

"Could be anytime now." Ordelia shrugged, polishing a dining table carved from the first oak in the grove to fall by lightning strike.

Louise unfolded a black tablecloth, pursing her lips together. *Odie is going to be around for many years yet*, she muttered. Over the cloth they laid colorful settings of fuchsia, orange, and green. Each plate had a set of silverware as old as the cemetery itself. Louise laid candles out, lighting all but one black pillar.

Around them, colorful picnic quilts waited for the other invited guests. A small table near the wall was covered in warming catering trays. The heavy fragrances quickened her heart. Smoke grated against the back of her throat, and she coughed into a stream of incense.

"You have to be able to taste the air," Ordelia reminded her. "If you cannot, the spirits cannot, and they will not come to feast."

"Will our guest?" Louise wondered. She dug her thumbnail nervously into her fingertips. She would be the one to welcome him. The thought made her lightheaded, and she clutched the back of a chair.

"It is not just the food that will entice him," Ordelia snorted, staring again at the dress. She had modernized it slightly for Louise's body, taking the mulberry wool in, but the effect was stunning. She lowered the shoulders on the bodice a little more, her hands hesitating inches from Louise's cheeks. "You don't have to do this."

Louise pressed a softened hand to her face. "I would do anything for you."

"There's no guarantee it will work," Ordelia warned sadly.

And no guarantee I'll make it through alive, Louise finished. She'd known that from the beginning. They both had.

"He will come," she grinned breathlessly, adrenaline pulsing through her muscles. "He cannot refuse us."

The old woman lashed out and slapped the feverish

glint from Louise's eye. Louise covered the sting with her hand, flushing angrily. "You hit me!"

"Keep your wits about you! That dog is dangerous."

"But you said he can't hurt us."

"Not tonight. But don't go looking at his pretty face and forgetting that tomorrow comes soon after today." Ordelia glanced up at the darkening sky with sharp eyes. "Our guests will be on their way soon. It's time." She thrust a large clunky bottle into Louise's hand and disappeared into the edges of dark.

"That's some pep talk." Louise's full hands trembled. She returned to the entrance, her long skirt teasing the ground. She pulled energy up from the earth as she moved. It surged up through her muscles into her stomach and into her heart. The excess fluttered there, battering against bone.

In the iron gateway of the small family plot, Louise pulled the old cork from the rum bottle, gently swirling the liquor in the bottle. It's aged, pungent perfume added to the sensory dance. Thick smoke took shadow forms as spirits stirred around her.

Louise stared into the spreading inky night, overwhelmed by all the fragrances. She let it wash over her body and shook it off, breathing deeply. She focused her thoughts on one figure, one form, and one name.

"There is a place for you at our family table tonight. I invite you in. I entice you to come with the last of my great-granddaddy's secret stash, bought off a witch doctor's back porch in Jamaica when he was young." Louise heard whispers rising within the walls behind her. She tipped the bottle towards the ground. "Come, old man, or I'll gift your share to the earth."

"No need wasting good spirits on those who no longer have lips with which to taste it." His voice was smoke lifting from the dirt. Louise gasped. Swirling shadows molded a formless shape, but it was a man who stepped into the light. His dark, unmarred skin stretched sleekly over the curves of his bones like silk. He was luminously beautiful, stepping forward into her silence as she fell into the glittering galaxies of his eyes. He grinned. "Just who are you calling Old Man?"

Louise blinked back into her body as a blush crept up her neck. She cursed inwardly, grateful for the sting still on her cheek. Odie was right. She gripped the dark rum. "Hello, Crossroads Man."

"I'd be glad for a sip of that." The man chewed on his lip from the other side of the gate.

"So you accept my invitation?" she pressed. The

words were important.

"And whose invitation would I be accepting?"

"My name is Louisa Angeline." Her voice strengthened with the sound of her birth name.

"Louisa Angeline," he grinned. "How could I resist such a treat? I gladly accept."

Louise poured the rum into two shot glasses pulled from a nearby column and thrust one at her guest. She thrilled to be face to face with such a being. He maintained eye contact with her as he took the offering, running his pinky finger along the outside of her hand. An electric shock shot down her spine, and she bit the inside of her cheek. *Do not be fooled by his glamour.*

The man rolled the shot glass across his bottom lip before tipping the heady rum back greedily. His eyelids fluttered, and he licked his lips, reaching for the second shot. Louise shook her head.

"The first one is for the Crossroads Man. The second one is for the spirits walking the world." She set the shot glass on top of the column at the gate as he took a step closer to her. His breath smelled like jasmine and mushrooms and salted sea spray.

"Dinner is ready!" Ordelia yelled behind them as Louise jumped away. The man smiled wickedly. He held out his arm until Louise took it. She frowned internally. *He knows his magic is palpable.*

"A beautiful setting," he intoned slyly as she pulled him towards the table. "Very intimate."

"It's a private cemetery," Louise explained, taking her hand from his arm. Odie paced them in the shadows. It gave her comfort.

The Crossroads Man bent down to snag a pinch of dirt, which he touched to his tongue. "This land is old."

"It's very old." Louise gestured to the finely carved black chair at the head of the table. "The place of honor belongs to you, Crossroads Man." She hesitated. "Is there a better name I could call you? Anything I can think of seems to diminish you somehow." *And names are important.*

His smile stretched to meet the starlight, as she hoped it might. He pulled smartly at the cuff of his old suit jacket, waiting to be seated. "For such flattery, you may call me whatever you wish. For tonight."

"What about Frederick?" Louise asked, sweeping behind his chair. A small muscle twitched at his temple but smoothed quickly. She grinned, pulling the chair out. "No, not something so mundane as Frederick," Louise slid the chair in beneath him with a flourish, leaning low, trying to sound more clever than she felt. "Welcome to our table, Shadow." The dark man winked his delight, and the old woman snorted from the food table.

Louise turned her back and walked slowly to the other end of the table, scowling. *Shadow?* She might as well have named him Rumpelstiltskin.

The young hostess smoothed the fabric where the bodice met her skirt, noting how Shadow's gaze followed her fingertips across her hips. She smiled shyly and picked up a small wooden box. Beneath Shadow's gaze, she felt far more naked than she did in her normal clothes. Exhaling, the girl born Louisa Angeline steadied her hands and pulled a match from the pewter box, striking the tip on the ornate handle.

"You are a mighty fire. Burn bright with me. Together we will tend the lighthouse to guide the ancestors home." She stared into the small flame before lifting it to the wick of the unlit black candle at her end of the table. The candle flared to life, and the other lights in the cemetery flickered in unison. Louise stood on the bones of her family dead and pulled the echo of life up through the stone and earth, up through the soles of her shoes, up through her living bones, into her heart, and into her voice. She could feel Odie mirroring her from behind Shadow's chair. A strange wind ate the flame that remained on the match. "May it be so."

"May it be so," Shadow echoed respectfully. "I deeply appreciate you inviting me to share in such an affair."

"We've wanted to invite you for generations," Louise smiled, her eyes shining. "It took us a while to collect the right ingredients—event, moon phase, recipes. It had to be perfect."

"With a perfect hostess, Louisa?" Shadow leaned forward.

She shrugged, holding contact with his dark eyes. "I fit the dress."

Ordelia stepped in from the dark, carrying a red platter covered with rich, steaming bread. She set it down beside Shadow. In close quarters, the braided bread's rich aroma of cinnamon and anise overwhelmed the cloud of incense.

"It is tradition to offer the first piece of pan de muerto to the visiting spirits," Ordelia smiled. She broke off a piece with whispered words of prayer before handing it to their guest.

"I assure you this offering is warmly received." Shadow nodded to Ordelia and raised his eyes to Louise, lifting the bread to inhale its fragrance, "though I am far more than simple spirit."

"Of that I am sure, Shadow." Louise watched as he bit into the bread. With one zealous sweep of his long fingers, he folded the rest of it into his mouth. The young dark-haired woman relaxed back in her chair. *At last the ruse is over.* "Well?"

"It is the most flavorful bread I have ever received." He reached for another piece. "Merci."

"It's the least we could do for you, Old Man," Louise sat up straighter as the breeze spoke lowly in her ear. It was time. "Thank you for answering my summons."

"Oh, so you summoned me now?" Shadow Man's eyes twinkled with sharp little edges as he bit into the second piece of bread. "With your mighty powers? You invoked me, and now I have to do your bidding, is that it?"

"No. Of course not," Louise assured him, counting the passing seconds quietly in her head. Both Louise and Ordelia watched as a veil fell over his gaze and an ashen cloud moved behind his eyes. His smooth brow furrowed. A strange crease broke the line of his face and the younger woman no longer thought him pretty. Louise could see the thing that lurked beneath the mask. She teased it. "Does it not please you?"

"No." Shadow spat the bread out.

"You must not have gotten the recipe right," Ordelia feigned confusion.

"I did! Let's see, there's milk and butter," Louise tilted her head, counting the ingredients off with her fingers, "sugar, salt, yeast, water, eggs, flour, anise and cinnamon." Shadow narrowed his eyes as she smiled. "And also basil, bay, nettle, rosemary, sage, mullein, nightshade and just a hint of asafoetida."

"You dare feed me devil's dung?!" Fire filled Shadow's eyes. He tried to raise himself from the chair with a wild roar quickly eaten by the thick trunks of oak trees. He paled as his arms and legs refused his commands. Louise and Ordelia silently watched his futile struggle, enraging him further. His face contorted in fury as he attempted to lunge at them. All he managed was a light sweat. He was trapped to his chair.

"It worked." Louise grinned at the old woman, pulling the shoulders of her bodice back up. "You were right about how much copal we'd need to burn to mask the smell."

"Of course I was right," Ordelia snickered. "I've been planning this my whole life."

"What have you done?!" Spittle flew from Shadow's mouth.

The Fragrant Feast   85

Louise pulled the wig off her head with an exaggerated flair, running her hands through her short pixie cut. "I invited you to feast with my family dead. And you accepted."

"Under false terms!" Shadow blackened.

Louise frowned. "No. I *am* Louisa Angeline. This *is* my family cemetery. This costume is as much a part of me as the one you wear. My friends call me Lou, but you can call me Louise."

Shadow flailed embarrassingly against the magic holding him still, to no avail. His nostrils flared. "Witch!!"

"Everything I know my Gran taught me," she said sweetly as Ordelia stepped beside her. "The pan de muerto is her special recipe." She patted the old woman's hand proudly. "I would like to introduce you to Ordelia Grace Lozier."

"Lozier?" The man asked as the name tugged at a strange memory.

"I did not think to, after all this time, but I know your face," Ordelia whispered, approaching him. There was no malice in her voice.

"What have you done to me?"

"We made you into a spirit magnet. The herbs in your gut are tethered to the herbs bundled beneath the chair you sit on, a chair those hands you borrow carved." Ordelia's eyes flashed. "The bones you wear remember this land. And that face is no longer yours to bear."

"Bruja!" he spit.

"I am curandera, as is my granddaughter. We are healing this land, healing our family."

Shadow shook his head. "Impossible."

"I think you want to believe that," Louise leaned across the table at their prisoner as Ordelia disappeared behind the central tombstone.

"You got one up on me," Shadow chuckled uncomfortably. "I respect that. Okay, you win. I'll be your djinn. What is it you would ask of me? It is yours, anything, if you set me free."

"Like I can trust you." Louise laughed.

"It's not about trust. It's about power." He wilted in the chair. "And you have it."

Louise stood uncertainly. Was there an easier answer? "Anything?"

"Ask what you will of me," Shadow entreated. His eyes were wells of pain and suffering.

Another glamour. She wasn't going to fall for it, but they'd worried needlessly. *So this is the monster we've been hunting? What is so dangerous about a creature kept immobilized by a bundle of garden herbs?*

"Louisa!" Ordelia exclaimed, slamming an old skull down hard on the table. Louise jumped away in confusion, staring at the hand that had been a half-inch away from touching his flesh. Shadow winked at her. "Foolish girl!"

Louise lifted her heavy skirt and crossed back to her grandmother with an apologetic frown. Her body felt strange, as if a thousand small leeches had been feeding from it. Ordelia dusted off the top of the skull with a bit of cloth, muttering under her breath.

"Am I supposed to know who that is?" Shadow narrowed his eyes. Ordelia turned her backside to him, and raised an eyebrow at Louise.

"I warned you."

"You did, Odie."

"If I had been a year older and a minute longer retrieving this..." Ordelia shuddered. "That was it, the moment I was dreading. The moment I might have lost you." She poked Louise hard in the ribs. "Don't do that again."

Louise nodded. "Are you ready, Gran?"

Tears glistened in Ordelia's eyes. She had been

training her whole life for one night of magic. And she had trained Louise. They each pulled out a small leather pouch they'd squirreled into their pockets.

"What are you doing?" Shadow demanded. He sounded miles away.

Louise stood, staring into her grandmother's eyes. Her ancestress' skull sat on the table between them. Louise breathed energy up from the earth as Odie breathed it down from the moon. With the next inhalation, they switched, taking hands. The moon energy pried at the edges of Louise's body.

When she could no longer sense where she ended and her grandmother began, she emptied her pouch into her hand. Odie did the same. Louise held a clear crystal sphere, glittering with hundreds of thin, golden filaments. Ordelia's orb was quartz with thick black crystals.

"Now is the time," Louise chanted, sliding her golden crystal into the right socket of the skull. The flames around the cemetery grew brighter.

"The time is now," Ordelia answered. Their guest struggled against his trap.

"You wouldn't," Shadow hissed. Ordelia held her black sphere up before the empty left socket. The crossroads man paled. "Wait!"

The side of Ordelia's mouth curled up. "There will be no bargains tonight. You can leave that body willingly, or I will strip you from it one limb at a time."

"You don't want to do that." Shadow's grin was full of sharp teeth.

The old woman laughed. "Why not?"

"You would damage this vessel."

Ordelia's hand dropped a centimeter. She blinked. "Lafayette Lozier is long dead."

"Is he now?" Shadow met Ordelia's narrowed eyes and held her challenge. "Does he not smile at you? Do his teeth not flash in your direction?"

"You lie." There was angry anguish in her voice. The leaves on the oak trees stilled. The flames danced uncertainly. Louise grabbed onto the thread of the magic they meant to work, and the lights steadied.

"I do not," Shadow smiled smugly. "Or I would not inhabit him still. Dead flesh is of no use to me. There's another choice here."

Ordelia clenched her eyes shut, her heart swelling. An hour ticked by in three agonizing seconds. "Thankfully," she said, tears sliding across her cheeks, "it is not my decision to make." Ordelia pushed the second crystal into the skull. A wind whipped up as all the candle flames in the cemetery danced left and centered again. The copal smoke thickened, creating a ring around them. She raised her voice. "Now is the time!"

"The deal is off the table." Shadow's eyes turned black and their blackness seemed to pulse and push the dark outside of his body and into the air around him. Louise quavered. She could no longer see the candles on the other side of where he sat—

"The time is now!" Louise yelled. The orbs in the skull began to glow with an eerie green light. The air in the cemetery shifted, and she could taste dust in every particle of it. A roaring like migrating cicadas filled the small field as a bellowing spirit knocked on the wind.

Louise gripped Odie's hand. She pulled the energy up from the earth, like her grandmother had taught her. She pushed the energy through her body, into her arm and into her grandmother. Ordelia smiled beside her. The two women spoke in one voice.

"Rosella Marguerite Lozier! Beloved wife of Lafayette Frederick Lozier! We call you here to our table. We call you back to your bones. We call you here as judge against the creature that rides your husband's flesh!"

A disembodied female voice thundered through the cemetery. *<Jackal! Thief!>* The eyes in the skull flickered. *<Our family will feed you no more!>*

"Feed me?" Shadow challenged. "I take only what is mine to take. That this land belongs to your family is only because of the bargain your husband struck with me. Willingly." He glared at Louise, at where she held her grandmother's hand, where they channeled energy into the ether. "He was about to lose everything. Lafayette stood where the hunting trail crossed the dirt road into town and bargained with me that this land would provide for his family for generations. It was a mutual agreement."

<Liar!>

"You thought we wouldn't find out," Ordelia spat. "That we would never know, that we'd just think Lafayette slunk out on his family. But my daddy knew the truth."

<You made a deal to claim him at the end of his life. His natural end.>

"But you didn't wait," Ordelia growled.

Louise watched as the devil man's stolen face froze. The candlelight flickered like lightning around them, il-luminating the hundred and thirty year-old skin. How many decades could the flesh slough off dead cells, rejuvenating them from beneath before what was left was no longer the person it had been?

"My great-great grandfather is tired, Shadow, and we are stronger than you," Louise added.

His face wrenched itself into a threatening scowl. "I am older than the demons, daughter."

"Not just me. I'm talking about generations of witches, on the night they can freely walk, beneath a blue moon. All of us." Louise could feel them solidifying in the smoke behind her, their mouths moving in a shared prayer, and a shared focus.

The skull flickered. *<Come to me, husband.>*

"Are you certain, Grandmother?" Ordelia's voice sounded small.

<I have seen what this one has done in my husband's skin, generations of feeding from the weakest of the earth and watching their ruination. If Lafayette lives within, waking him now would be cruel. Now is the time.>

"The time is now," a hundred voices answered, both dead and living. Shadow looked about wildly.

A deep bell tolled beyond the gate. Dozens of living men and women, old and young, uncles, and cousins, sisters and brothers, circled the cemetery, each holding a candle, adding light to the darkness and speaking the same long-learned prayer. Louise added her voice to the chorus, her tongue singing over the strange words. They were words of unbinding, of spirit separating from flesh. The devil man might not willingly leave the bones, but they would rescue Lafayette's spirit from his prison.

They invoked his name and called to his blood with their own. The Crossroad Man's tissue quivered, and he screamed. Louise extended the true invitation intended for the evening. She invited Lafayette Lozier to stay, and the man sleeping time away within Shadow responded.

The Crossroads Man began to convulse in his chair. The deep molecules of the tissue holding him dislodged him vehemently. Something tickled at her skin, and Louise laughed. He was reaching tethers out to the mob of descendants, seeking a new anchor, but he could not touch them. Louise smiled, drawing a worn leather bag out from inside her bodice. Ordelia grinned wickedly exposing her own leather warding bag.

His eyes widened in fright. Every person in the dark wore one as well. He couldn't touch any of them. He was lost. If he passed too much time without form, he risked becoming a true shadow; it was hard for ether to remember flesh. The old woman's face told him she knew that already.

"Lafayette Frederick Lozier." Half of the chorus in the cemetery began to chant his name.

"Cross over," the other half chanted in turn.

"Lafayette Frederick Lozier."

"Cross over."

Louise and Ordelia joined in the cry, their eyes turning a brilliant green. "Cross over!"

And their ancestor did. After millennia of walking the earth with borrowed feet, Crossroads Man's eyes narrowed in unwilling defeat. He threw the head he wore back and opened it wide.

Darkness crawled out, slowly, stretching like a long-slumbering cat as it mixed with the air. It recoiled from the lingering copal smoke, twisting and bending as it welled up from the mouth of the well-dressed man. It's only safe escape was up, far from hope of human habitation. The dark cloud fled to the sky with a roar, taking the essence of its host with it.

The Lozier descendants slowed their chanting until their voices stilled. Ordelia's younger siblings and their children, grandchildren, and great-grandchildren entered the cemetery, candles flickering in the All Hallows dark. They filled the cemetery, standing among the returning spirits, gathering around the table and watched as time tripped backwards over itself. The body of their ancestor decayed and shriveled until only mummified remains sat in the chair. A murky light hovered over the table, approaching the skull, floating closer to where Louise and Ordelia stood.

"Grandpa Lafayette?" Ordelia was awestruck.

The light enveloped the skull and changed its hue to match the glowing orbs. Louise could see how dank it was, still, compared to the other spirits that stood with them. She could see the weight of what he had seen. Even if the others couldn't see past their wonder, she could see it.

Her great-great grandmother Rosella Lozier's voice sighed around them one last time. *<Bury my husband with me and let us rest.>*

Ordelia bent to kiss the top of the skull, tears rolling silently down her cheeks. "It was good to hear your voice again." She removed the golden sphere from the socket. "Be at rest."

"Be at peace," everyone responded. The eyes ceased glowing.

Louise bent forward and kissed the cool bone. Her

tears wet the relic. She pulled the crystal from the skull. "Be at rest."

"Be at peace," everyone said. The candles winked and flickered as the air exhaled. The green light floated up, dissipating into the star light.

Louise closed her eyes, pushing the energy in her chest down through her body, down into the earth. She sent back what she no longer needed. Beside her Odie did the same, careful not to release too much or their muscles would feel like they'd been stretched through a wringer.

Family swept forward to remove the tainted bread from the table, producing a second fragrantly spiced loaf containing far fewer ingredients. Great-Uncle Frederick poked one of his grandsons to remove the herb bundles from under the chair.

"Louisa." Odie waited, holding the platter of un-broken bread out towards her. Louise floated across the grass and broke off the first offering. She laid it on the plate set before the true guest of honor. She stroked his cheek with the back of her hand lightly, touching him for the first and last time. He was per-fectly preserved.

One by one the living each broke off a bit and laid it

on the plate before Lafayette, as Great-Uncle Frederick stood before the monolith and began his yearly recitation of the names of the dead buried in the cemetery. His son Nicholas picked up his mandolin and plucked out a cheerful tune beneath the names.

Other instruments joined in as the names faded. The small space filled with laughter and the spirits danced among them. Louise felt a breeze tickle the hairs around her neck, and she smiled.

"Welcome home, Grandfather Lafee."

Sarah Lyn Eaton is a writer fond of magical realism and dystopias. She has previously published the stories "The White Sisters" in *What Follows* and "Hold the Door" in *The Northlore Series, Volume 1: Folkore,* as well as "Jar of Pickles" in the anthology *One Thousand Words for War.*

The Pendragon Crystal
Kath Boyd Marsh

"Are we the only ones up?" Morgan scanned the kitchen then stared at the old wizard. When he realized Myrlin was using magic, he almost forgot why he needed to talk to the Master Wizard alone. Since their arrival in the human realm six months ago, Myrlin had used no magic at all. Day by day he'd seemed to grow more and more like the confused old man he pretended to be for the humans on this plane.

The wizard flicked a hand at a drawer and the cupboard, sending spoons and bowls to settle on the counter for the twins when they came into the kitchen. Two plates plunked down next to the frying pan on the stove. Where Morgan's mother would sit for a hurried breakfast, a coffee cup already steamed beside a container of yogurt.

"For now it's only us." Myrlin hummed as he worked. Which was part of the problem. The wizard shouldn't be this relaxed. These past six months in the human 21st century were only a week in the Dragon

Realm. A week, was plenty of time for Uthur's soldiers to find Morgan and his family.

When Uncle Uthur had captured Morgan's father, Myrlin had gathered Morgan and the rest of his family, and they'd escaped from the palace. As soon as they'd all arrived in his crystal cave, Myrlin had ignored them all, sending rocks lifting and panels of crystals sliding while he hunted for something. "Help me, boy. We need the Pendragon Crystal to take back your father's throne."

Morgan scanned the crystal-encrusted walls of the cave. "I never heard of it. Not one of these, then?"

Myrlin had laughed. "Of course not." He'd thumped his head. "Of course *NOT*! We must go."

Morgan's mother, always the patient one, laid a slender dragon paw on the wizard's arm slowing his frantic pace. "Where do we need to go?"

"Away, of course. Long, long away. It's where I'd be if I were the crystal." Myrlin smiled and snapped his fingers. A purple stone appeared. "Crystal finder," he'd said. "Now a spell to send us on our way and bring us back successfully." He began the chant, having signaled Morgan, his mother, and his twin sisters Elaine and Evangeline to hold paws in a circle ending and beginning with

Myrlin, the most powerful wizard ever.

But his chant was only half-finished when the cave shook, sending them all to their knees. "Into human form at once!" Myrlin yelled. They shifted from royal dragons as he added, "And we are *Gone!*"

With that, they were indeed gone from the cave. Four dragons and a wizard stood in human form in a human house, in the human 21st century, the house they had now lived in for the past six months in Grove Township.

"We have to talk," Morgan started again, staring at Myrlin like he could force the elderly wizard to focus.

"Indeed? Do you wish your eggs and bacon crispy?" Myrlin cracked four eggs into a bowl and whirled a finger to beat them to a froth.

"Myrlin, we've been here too long, and there's no sign of this Pendragon Crystal. I don't get why a dragon crystal would be in the human world, but you said it would be at the high school, but ... nothing." Morgan tried to take the bowl out of Myrlin's hands, but the old man was surprisingly strong and kept hold of it.

Myrlin grinned. "No sign of Uthur. Good, eh?"

"No, not good. I need to get back. To save my father."

Morgan let go of the bowl and leaned against the counter.

Myrlin snapped his fingers. Bacon flew out of the refrigerator and slapped into the heated pan. He turned to Morgan. "I am sorry. You won't believe me, but your father is dead. Until you can return with an army, there is no point in going back. You, as the legitimate heir to the Dragon Realm, and your family would be slaughtered." The wizard's eyes had none of the fuzzy dreaminess they often held in this easy world of humans.

Morgan knew through his last scale that Myrlin was right. It had been possible to deny that his father was dead as long as the wizard behaved like a distracted elderly human, but Myrlin's old clarity was back, as was his keen logic. Uthur would never keep his brother Arthur alive.

"So it will do no good to find the crystal?" Morgan said, watching fat bubble and dance above the frying pan. If there was one thing dragons loved, it was bacon.

Myrlin turned and waved a hand over the splattering bacon, and the grease bounced off an invisible shield, raining back down into the pan. Morgan stood up straight. He had to make the wizard treat him like an adult. Talk to him.

Morgan knew Myrlin was back to his pre-escape wizard self, because of this magic, the first he'd done since they'd arrived. If you didn't count arranging for their home and neighbors who seemed to think the 'Smythes' had always lived in Grove Township. Of course you had to add in how easily Mother had gotten her job as crops supervisor for the Food for Life charity. It was the perfect job for his mother who would have overseen dragon farmers if the wife of the Dragon King was allowed such a job. If Morgan became King, he'd make sure all the old-fashioned rules about who could do what were broken.

A part of Morgan felt like a traitor for adjusting so easily to life as a human high school junior. His natural dragon ability to swim made him the captain of the swim team a week after school had begun, and his good grades came naturally. He felt a bit guilty about how much he liked being around his new friend Chrys. Not that he had done anything about it, since feeling this way about a human female was totally forbidden.

Myrlin waved at Morgan to sit, and he found himself plopped on his stool. The wizard's eyes were hawk-bright when he said, "We will discuss everything this afternoon when you and I will have private time."

When Morgan objected, Myrlin waved a hand and continued, "Your sisters have their music lessons. Your mother will be late because of meetings with donors. And your swim practice will be cancelled."

Morgan did not argue. Myrlin was finally acting like the king's counselor, the wizard who knew the future.

"The Crystal will find you today," Myrlin added then said in a louder voice, "How are my favorite dragonelles?" The elderly wizard's loopy smile was back as Morgan's twin sisters galloped into the kitchen. The pair, no matter how much trouble they might get into otherwise, were perfect princesses around their 'uncle' Myrlin. They loved him so much, maybe even more now that they thought he was just a regular old man and not a scary wizard. They rushed up to him, plastering kisses on his wrinkled cheeks and hugging him with all their little princess strength.

Elaine wrinkled her nose. "I don't eat meat!" She pointed at the bacon.

Evangeline nodded.

"Don't worry, my little angels, your special cereal awaits." He pointed to their bowls, and as they turned to clamber up on their stools, he started to wave his hand in his summoning-way, catching Morgan's stare. Myrlin shook his head, dropped his hand, and waddled to the refrigerator to pull out milk to pour on the cereal.

Morgan lifted an eyebrow. Whatever was happening was definitely just between Myrlin and him. For now the wizard continued not using magic in front of the rest of the family. Morgan wished they'd had another few minutes alone, so he could ask about the army Myrlin said was connected to the Crystal, the army to defeat his uncle. This afternoon seemed too long to wait to ask.

Mother joined the breakfast group, and normal twin chaos reigned until she left for work. Morgan dropped the girls at their school before he drove on to Grove Township High.

When Morgan saw Chrys, he forgot all about ... everything. He couldn't get words straight. Which was so messed up. He was a dragon prince hanging out in human form, and she was a human. There was no way he should want to date her. And now that Morgan hoped Myrlin was ready to drop the human act and really help find the crystal, there would be no time for ... anything.

"Hi, Morgan," Chrys said walking beside him as

they headed to their Analytical Geometry class. "Did you meet the new guy?"

There was something odd in her voice. She'd been mildly flirty before, but now the lightness in her tone was gone. Her question sounded too serious for her words.

"No. Who?"

"He's joined the swim team. Funny name. Mordie Pendragon. Same as yours." Her mouth snapped shut. "I mean unusual." But her eyes were pinned on Morgan's.

As far as anyone knew here in the human realm, his last name was Smythe. No one should know he was a Pendragon. Before he could ask her how ... a male as dark-haired as Morgan was blonde, and as tall as Morgan, who looked familiar and yet not, strode down the hall headed straight at them. The new guy had a smirk on his face. Shocked, Morgan kept his mouth snapped shut and his face as blank as possible. This human: his attitude, the dark gray eyes, the half moon birthmark, it was all a younger echo of the dragon Uthur, Morgan's uncle and his father's murderer. Had his cousin tracked him down?

Morgan paid no attention to Chrys's next words. Humans were no longer important. Time had run out.

Uthur had sent his son to hunt Arthur's son, and he had found him.

But the first words out of Mordie's mouth confused Morgan. He was focused on Chrys, not Morgan. "Well, if it isn't the fair Chrys. Is this your boyfriend? I know you have one, or you would not have turned me down." He grinned at her like this was a teasing joke, but when he looked at Morgan his eyes were cold.

Mordred had to know. Morgan didn't want to break out in dragon on dragon battle in front of humans. If Uthur's son knew he had found the missing prince, Morgan would make sure Mordred also knew there was going to be a battle. He stepped forward. "I'm Morgan—"

Chrys interrupted, stepping between the two males. "Smythe. I did mention a boyfriend, didn't I? Did I say that we'd been sweet on each other since we were five?" She snagged Morgan's hand. "He doesn't like me to say, but when we were little our mothers put us in the same wading pool, both of us without a stitch of clothing!" She laughed like this was incredibly funny.

Morgan was too surprised at her facile lie to speak. For months now they'd talked casually; flirting humans called it. But, boyfriend? He looked at Mordred, who wore a puzzled look as if he thought he was wrong about something.

Had Mordred suspected he'd found Morgan, but human Chrys's insistence she'd known Morgan for years convinced him that Morgan wasn't ... Morgan? Since dragons never used human form on the dragon plane, Mordred had no sure way to know Morgan's human form was the prince dragon he sought.

At the very least Chrys had confused Mordred. Why had she lied?

Probably the special soap Myrlin made the family bathe in to cover the dragon scent had something to do with Mordred not realizing he'd found his prey. Apparently the soap didn't just hide dragon scent from humans, but worked on other dragons. Human form or not, Morgan could definitely smell the sulfur of Mordred's flame stomach. Which meant he had used his fire on something or someone and not long ago.

This was not the time to hide. If Mordred was out torturing or killing to find Morgan, what kind of coward was Morgan if he hid? He'd face Uthur's killer son.

He started to shake Chrys's hand free, but she held on harder, harder than he thought a human girl could grip. But that was probably because she was the best swimmer in the female events. She had to be strong. Deciding it might be a good idea to not create a confrontation that might set Mordred into full flaming battle mode, maybe turning the school to a smoldering pile of cinders, Morgan let Chrys drag him into the math classroom. He'd find a way to track Mordred and confront him where there wouldn't be human casualties.

But Mordred followed them, sitting in the lone empty seat on the other side of the room. Throughout class, Morgan slid looks at Mordred. Finally, Chrys scribbled a note, dropped it on the floor, and as she picked it up, stuffed it in Morgan's sneaker. He would have laughed, but this was no time to attract Mr. Potvin's attention. Morgan sneezed and managed to bend over far enough to retrieve the note. If their math teacher couldn't figure out what they were up to, he really did need new glasses.

Chrys had written: "We need to talk after school. Stop staring at Mordred! You'll give yourself away!"

Unable to stop himself, Morgan turned and stared at her. This was impossible. She knew about him? She knew about the real him?

When Analytical Geometry was over, Morgan took Chrys's arm and hissed in her ear. "I need to talk to you."

"No duh," she said and walked with him. "You go in the boys locker room, I'll go through the girls and meet you in Coach's office. Wait for me. No matter what, don't follow me!" She gave him a look as steely as his own father's.

Before he could ask, she speed-walked down the hall and took a turn the opposite direction from the locker rooms. Why was she headed straight for the pool entrance?

When Mordred followed her, Morgan hesitated. He smelled the stench of killer flames on Mordred. He wanted Chrys dead? Morgan didn't care what this female said, it was his duty as Prince Morgan to protect. He would not let his cousin do … anything.

Morgan set off after the pair, but was stopped by the swim coach. Helpless to follow, he watched Mordred look both ways then follow Chrys through the pool doors.

Coach put a hand out toward Morgan's arm, then withdrew it. He knew it wasn't because Coach sensed there were scales beneath the human skin, but that teacher-humans avoided touching pupils. For dragons personal touch was reserved for those you were closest to or trying to kill. And a bite could be fatal or grant an unchangeable bond and dragon-life to creatures other than dragons, the closest thing to eternal life.

Coach's words brought Morgan back to the moment. "Practice has been cancelled. Can you let the rest of the team know? I have to get busy rescheduling."

He nodded, but Coach was already shuffling files and trudging down the hall toward his office. There was no time; Morgan ran as fast as his human legs would allow. When he skidded through the pool doors, at first he didn't see anyone. It was so silent the bubbles bursting from the pool aerator sounded like fireworks.

Then shadows wavered beyond the far end of the pool where the overhead lights had gone out. He headed toward them. Halfway around the pool, a blast of light, maybe from Chrys's cellphone, showed her backed up to a wall and Mordred morphed into his gray-scaled dragon form. There was no mistaking Mordred's son in the dark gray sheen of scales only a shade lighter than his eyes.

Mordred was going to kill the girl! There was no other way he'd reveal his dragon form, unless he meant to bite her and … claim her for his own. The problem was Mordred looked too calm for it to be murder. Dragons and humans did not mix, which was why Morgan fought his feelings for Chrys, but Mordred and his father had long been suspected of the Dark Magics. Would they want a human slave?

When Mordred finally lunged at Chrys, Morgan roared and shifted into his red and purple scales. Myrlin would just have to deal with the mess of a human finding out. There was no way Morgan, Prince of the Dragon Realm, would let Uthur's get kill or enslave a human right in front of him.

Mordred jerked at the roar, and his eyes flared with a rim of killer red.

Chrys yelled, "You fool!"

Mordred whipped back to her, swept his tail and pulled her against his side. With a look of scarlet-glinting triumph, he clamped down on her neck.

Morgan spewed flame, scorching Mordred's back and making him jerk away from Chrys. She ducked and darted from him. Morgan watched her race up the bleachers and jump to the balcony. Satisfied that she was out of the dragon's reach for the moment, he switched his attention back to Mordred.

"Crap!" Mordred stalked along the pool deck, crimson glowing at his nostrils, his eyes now more than half red. "I knew it!" he growled. "The girl tried to confuse me, but I knew it."

"Good for you," Morgan said as he gathered his own

fire to battle Mordred's. Another reason for Myrlin to be angry: Morgan had let himself be tracked down. The question now was whether Mordred had come alone or had an army of Uthur's soldiers come with him? And if they had, where were they? Morgan thought of his unaware family. "So you do this all by yourself? Or you got an army to back you up, coward?" He hoped to make his furious cousin spew out information.

The gray dragon stopped ten yards away. That smirking smile pulled on Morgan's sharp-fanged dragon snout. "Worried about your family, princeling?"

"No. You got lucky finding me. No way you know where my family is." But how had Mordred even come to Grove Township?

"It's my fault," Chrys called. "He tracked me."

For a second Morgan tried to understand how tracking a human girl had helped Mordred. In that second, Mordred blasted flame so wide and tall there was no way to dodge it. There was only one defense. Morgan spit out the flame he had left to counteract the attack, but there hadn't been enough time to replenish. His flame only shot out ten feet and died.

A flash streaked in front of him. A pure silver dragon hovered between him and Mordred's flames. Its wings spread wide, the Silver (one of the legendary warrior tribe that were pledged to no king and battled anyone who crossed them) took the blow of the flames and dropped to the pool deck.

Morgan did not have time to rush to the silver dragon. He did not have flames. He had only the one thing he did better than any other dragon, and which he hadn't done in six months. He flew. He flew as fast as he'd ever done in any of the tournament races. He pictured the speed of light and threw himself at Mordred before the other dragon could recharge his flame.

Talons out, Morgan ripped Mordred's gullet from snout to heart zone, and his cousin dropped like a sack of stones. The wound was not necessarily mortal; if he got back to the dragon realm fast enough, he could heal. But Mordred would not fight again for a long time.

Morgan scanned for that army. His gaze fell on the silver dragon struggling to get on her feet. He leaned over her. Her burns were in her heart, mortal wounds. Only a dragon bite could save her. But if he did this, he would be forever bound to her. Since he would never take a slave, this meant they'd be wed one day. He'd never thought to make this promise so soon, but who would he rather spend his life with someday than a dragon so brave she would give her life for him?

He bent and tenderly bit into the Silver's slowly pulsing throat. His saliva washed into her. He waited holding on. Could he do enough? A royal bite was supposed to—

"Okay, make-out king, you can cut it out now!" the raspy but snarky voice coming from the silver dragon sounded very familiar.

Morgan sat back staring. "You?"

"Quick, aren't you? We've been watching you for … six months." Chrys, the silver dragon sat upright.

"We?"

"I take it Myrlin failed to mention the Warriors of the Silver Guard are the army you need?" Her eyes pinned him as he shook his head. "And he didn't mention that we were keeping watch on you and your family?"

He shook his head again.

Chrys, the Silver, sighed. "I think sometimes Myrlin is getting … a little forgetful?"

Morgan laughed. "Most assuredly. But …" He frowned. "He said today I would find the Crystal we need to gather the army, return, and defeat Uthur." He pointed at her. "Do you know where it is?"

The Silver morphed into the human form of Chrys.

"Really? I have to explain this to you? Chrys. Chrystal?"

"Okay." He tried to look like he'd already put that together. "But why the wait? You introduced yourself to me the first day of school. Why wait to reveal yourself and almost die at Mordred's hands?"

"I think Myrlin will answer that one. It was his plan." She dusted off her jeans and looked at the bleeding Mordred. "We need to get him out of here. No way can we explain a dying dragon."

"He won't die. Royals don't die unless you pierce their hearts." Morgan looked down at the gray dragon and scowled. "But you're right; we will have to get him out of here unnoticed." He looked up at the skylights, open over the pool, huge wide windows that a couple of dragons could navigate.

Chrys sighed and morphed back to dragon. "Okay. Where do we take him?"

"I think to Myrlin. So home." Morgan grabbed a towel and stuffed it onto Mordred's chest to staunch the blood. He took Mordred's head and Chrys took his feet. He was pretty sure if he let a Silver take Mordred by the head, there might accidentally be some neck-breaking by the time they got to Myrlin.

They were airborne and above the giant skylights

as a group of students flowed into the pool area. No one should have been coming to the pool area since the parctice was cancelled. One of them looked up as Morgan beat his wings to break for the skies. The boy grabbed hold of another.

"Oh, no," Chrys said. "That's his army. Fly like you never flew before."

"Keep up!" Morgan spit, as he beat his wings and grabbed Mordred lower on his body in case she let go. They were over the first tree-line before he heard the other dragon wings following. She'd been right.

"Distraction," Chrys said.

He was afraid she was going to use herself, but she said it louder, and two silver dragons broke from the trees and headed back toward the chasing dragons.

"Your army?" Morgan asked.

"Yours," she said. "We're almost there. Slow down, and let's be sure this is not a trap."

They landed in the woods on the other side of Morgan's house. Chrys tied Mordred with Virginia Creeper vines and kicked him in the head. "To make sure he sleeps," she said, but she grinned.

Morgan tried not to smile too. They shifted to human form, better to slide unnoticed through the trees on foot.

When they were at the edge of the woods, they stopped and listened. "Three in the house," Chrys held up her fingers. "I count three heartbeats."

"Plus Myrlin," he said. "Who is as usual talking too much. And is he ... cooking?"

They looked at each other and shook their heads in mystification. For a moment more they listened. No other voices, no other hearts beating. All accounted for including the three who must be Mordred's men.

"How are we going to sneak up?" Chrys asked. "They can hear as well as we can."

"I think that's why Myrlin's keeping up the non-stop chatting, to distract. Let's go."

They ran across the grass and slipped in the back and up the basement steps. The door to the kitchen was cracked open. Morgan saw the three dragons, carefully keeping their wings tucked, drooling at the food that was being prepared, but not letting go of the swords they had drawn from their scabbards.

Before Morgan could think of a way to get in, Myrlin said, "Could one of you go down into the basement refrigerator?" He pointed at the kitchen refrigerator. "Like this one but at the foot of the basement steps. There should be a whole two pounds of bacon to go with the pancakes. I thought maybe I'd put bacon in the pancakes." Dragons were fools for bacon.

Morgan and Chrys hurried down the stairs and waited for the dragon to come down. But two stomped down the steps arguing. "Mordred said to kill the wizard. Why aren't we?"

The other, now at the refrigerator said, "Because he can cook bacon. How long since you've eaten?"

The other dragon shrugged and moved in on the first, elbowing him to get to the bacon.

As the two stood for a moment in front of the refrigerator, Chrys and Morgan clobbered them with iron poles from a stack beside the stairs.

"We need to bind them," Chrys said. "But without Virginia Creeper vine ..."

"You'll have to settle for a spell." Myrlin's voice came from the top of the steps. He snapped his fingers, and the two enemy dragons were covered in ropes of cold-fire.

Chrys and Morgan hurried up the steps. The third dragon was face down on the kitchen counter, snoring.

The wizard smiled. "I suppose he should have asked if it was pepper or cinnamon that I put in the pancakes." He snapped his fingers, and this dragon was bound in cold-fire. "I take it you have Mordred?"

"Yes. *And* I have a lot of questions," Morgan said.

"After." Myrlin pointed to the kitchen clock. "Your mother and sisters will return in three hours. Enough time to usurp the usurper. Right?"

Morgan looked at Chrys and then at Myrlin. "Well..."

"Look outside," Myrlin and Chrys said together.

On the lawn a hundred silver dragons stood, spread-wing to spread-wing. A sound like the song of the wind before a tornado worked up its fearful destruction gathered louder and louder as the dragons stomped and spit flame.

"You've proved yourself to be the proper successor to Arthur," Chrys said. "So the Warriors of the Silver Guard will fight for your kingdom."

"Proper because I bit you?" Morgan smiled.

"Why of course, you dummy." Chrys smiled as she led the way outside.

"She's going to be a handful as Queen, don't you think?" Myrlin said.

Morgan laughed. "You know it. But I can handle ..."

Myrlin held up a finger. "Don't finish that. No male dragon has ever 'handled' a Silver Warrior. You make her your ally, your companion, you earn her respect, but you never *handle* her."

Morgan nodded, morphed to dragon and stepped out to co-lead the Silver Warriors and regain the Dragon Throne.

At seven years old **Kath Boyd Marsh** self-published her first fantasy on lined notebook paper, stapled together by her grandfather, and starring a creature based on her little sister—the 'PB.' Before Kath moved to Richmond, KY to write about dragons, wizards, and other fantastic creatures, she lived in seven states, Panama, and one very haunted house. *The Lazy Dr'gon and the Bumblespells Wizard* was her debut novel.

Technological Magic

Susan Bianculli

When humans finally colonized the Moon in 2137, all Earth rejoiced that one of Mankind's oldest dreams had been achieved. When the colonists had finished building the infrastructure, they then began to do what humans have always done: have children. Though the adults had been the first extraterrestrial colonists, it was Amalthea and the children born on the Moon who were the first true extraterrestrial humans. They grew up attuned to the sounds of the colony station in a way their parents could never be; so when the familiar thrums that underlined their everyday existence changed, the children noticed.

"Did you hear that?" Amalthea asked, opening her eyes where she sat.

She and the twenty-one other teens sitting together in the Contemplation Studio had been doing a guided group meditation, but everyone had stopped concentrating at the exact same moment.

"Yeah, I did," said her friend Deimos. "Computer,

off." The soothing voice that had been conducting their mental exercises vanished.

All the other teens started talking over each other about what they'd heard. Amalthea called for silence, got it, and tapped her parents' code on her wrist computer.

"Dad? Mom? Did you just hear that?"

"Hear what?" her father replied through the speaker.

"Can you describe it?" her mother chimed in.

"I, uh, dunno. The background noises just went kinda off. We heard a change."

Amalthea could hear the frown in her father's voice. "I'll need more than that, young lady."

"I heard it too, Mr. Richard, Mrs. Jane," Deimos leaned over and added helpfully.

"Do you have a better description, Deimos?" asked Jane.

"Well, no …," he replied, his voice trailing off.

Jane inhaled sharply, and Richard said hurriedly, "We'll look into it," as he cut the connection short.

"No, the Chief Engineer wasn't being at *all* suspicious just then," a boy named Suttung said sarcastically.

"There's definitely something going on," Amalthea agreed.

"Should we investigate too?" Deimos asked.

"Investigate what and where, exactly?" Suttung asked. "We don't know what could be wrong, and the Moon colony is a huge place. It could be anywhere and anything."

"Maybe we should get into our space suits?" a girl named Bestla said.

"Why?" Deimos answered. "If the station implodes or anything, it's not like Earth would send up a rescue ship for the survivors."

All the teens exchanged solemn glances. Getting Mankind to colonize space had proven beyond the capabilities of the Earth's governments, so it had fallen, like so much had, to privatization. Eventually many of the smaller religious organizations had come together under the umbrella name Ancient Faiths Association and pooled their cash to achieve the space dream. But since the station was a privately funded enterprise it had always been understood that, despite the pride that the average Earth citizen had in the Moon colonists, no government down there would stir to rescue them if a life-threatening problem happened. That this could be an issue had never even crossed the teens' minds—until now.

"Well, we can't just sit around here," Amalthea said. "Let's split up to look around. Whether the adults like it or not, the more of us looking for something out of whack, the more chances it'll be found."

Everyone agreed, so Bestla projected a holo-map of the colony from her wrist computer into the center of the Contemplation Room so it could be divvied up among them. After a few confused minutes, eleven pairs of teens left for their self-assigned sectors.

"Come on, Amalthea! We have one of the furthest places to get to!" Deimos said.

"Let's grab a station scooter," Amalthea replied.

Stations scooters were communal property, so there were lots of them scattered all over the colony. Anyone could use one at any time as long as they knew how to drive. Deimos beat her to the last scooter and grabbed the driver's seat. Amalthea scrambled up behind him, and they sped down the hallways. After a few minutes, though, Deimos slowed to a stop.

"Deimos? What's wrong?" Amalthea asked.

"We haven't passed a single adult on our route, and we should have seen at least a dozen by now," he said with a frown.

"Hmmm. You're right." She scanned the empty

corridor. "Where is everyone?"

"Maybe they've already found out what's wrong and fixed it?" he suggested hesitantly.

"My Dad would have made a station-wide announcement in that case. Or at least told me about it, since I'm the one that brought it to his attention. And this place wouldn't be empty."

"Then maybe they've found out the problem and are having trouble fixing whatever it is?"

"But that still doesn't explain all the absences," Amalthea argued. "Parents of small babies should still be around, for example. And they're not."

"Hey, look, there's an adult," said Deimos.

Mrs. Sally, one of the teachers, was herding a big group of children across the corridor towards one of the playroom/gymnasium combinations. The group was made up of children from infancy to eight Earth rotations of age, with the older children leading the younger ones.

"That's not at all suspicious, either," Amalthea frowned. "Why are all those ages together like that? Where are Mrs. Sally's co-teachers, or the caretakers of the babies, at least? And where are the older kids?"

Mrs. Sally saw the pair of teens down the hall. Her

face scrunched up into a nervous expression as she called out to them. "You teens should be still in the Contemplation Room, shouldn't you? Your meditation exercises are not supposed to be done yet!"

"Mrs. Sally," Amalthea began, but Sally interrupted her.

"Sorry, I don't have time to chit-chat. I'm taking the youngsters for a special treat today. Go back to where you're supposed to be!" she ordered as the group disappeared into the gym.

Deimos started the scooter again. "I somehow don't think we'd get a straight answer if we try to ask her anything. We should get going on our search, pronto."

The pair finally reach their destination, which was the section with the astronomy lab. This part of the Moon base was located near the terminus line that separated the light half of the Moon from the dark half. A lot of transparent steel had been used in its making to afford the best view of the stars from different angles.

"Look!" Deimos said, torn between wonder and fear as he pointed out a see-through wall panel.

Outside, well into the dark side of the Moon, an amorphous *something* was fading in and out of sight. The question of where all the station personnel were was now answered because it seemed that nearly every adult was out there on the terminus line wearing space-suits and holding their hands out to it as if to physically stop the blob. What was even stranger was that some sort of energy was coming out of their hands to flood the area the shapeless thing kept trying to appear in!

"Do–do you see what I'm seeing?" Amalthea asked Deimos hesitantly.

"If you mean 'do I see a swirling rainbow-colored energy coming out of all the people we've known all our lives that is apparently stopping some sort of alien monster from materializing', then yeah, I do," he replied with disbelief.

The see-through wall they were looking through suddenly turned opaque as a familiar voice called out, "Amalthea? Deimos?"

The teens turned to see Amalthea's mother Jane removing her hand from a wall control panel before running down the corridor towards them.

"We're ...," Deimos began.

"I felt, errr, saw you approaching. Never mind whatever it is you're about to say. We need your help. Come on!"

"Mother! What's going on?!" Amalthea exclaimed.

"Get off that scooter, and I'll tell you as we go!"

Jane led them into the nearest set of laboratory rooms as she relayed to them a somewhat different version of the history than the one they'd been brought up with. Amalthea and Deimos were so shocked by what Jane told them that they remained silent until she'd finished speaking.

"I'm glad you two can understand what's going on now," Jane said when they'd reached the outside of the colony's northern-most airlock. "Get into the spare space suits here, and let's get out there! Two more fresh individuals might be just what we need!"

"Mother, we have to call in the other teens, at least," Amalthea demurred. "They deserve to know what's been going on, and it's only a matter of time before one of them finds out what's happening outside without having either you or us around to explain."

"And wouldn't having even more help be better anyway?" Deimos added.

Jane looked hesitant, but Amalthea filled her in on how the others were searching, and Jane nodded a reluctant acquiescence. Deimos quickly tapped a sub-circuit to reach the other teens and urge them to come, with spacesuits, to where he and Amalthea were.

"What?" and "Why?" were the responses he invariably received, but they each agreed to come, lured by the promise of information. Jane unwillingly left everything in their hands and went to rejoin the adults' endeavors. When the last of the other teens arrived at the airlock, Amalthea took a deep breath before letting loose the torrent of information she'd been entrusted with.

"Okay, everybody, listen up," she said. "We've a lot to tell you. One hundred years before the AFA that sent our parents here was formed, there had been hundreds of witches' covens, druids' groves, Norse circles, and whatnot all over Earth who'd been for years getting psychic indications of trouble. From casual talk after a public drumming circle, some of the groups found out that others had been having the same feelings of generalized danger. When enough leaders of neo-Pagan organizations had been made aware of the experiences, a call was put out to have people come together in a conference about it."

"Why're you talking about history?!" Bestla demanded. "You called us off the search for this?"

Deimos took up the tale. "Yeah, we did, Bestla, because what we're about to tell you changes everything we've thought we've known all our lives. *And* explains what started us on our search an hour ago. So, to continue: at the conference the attendees were stunned to find out that there were people who'd come who not only worshipped the old way, but *were* the old ways. They were real hereditary witches that could actually practice physical magic."

The other teens exchanged stunned looks.

"The hereditary witches asked for cooperation from everyone there in doing a full-on divination because they'd been unable to find out what was going on by themselves," he went on. "With everybody's energies helping, they were finally able to get the answer, which was chilling. The demons mentioned in such places as the works of John Dee and other historical manuscripts of witchcraft were getting ready to break through the Veil that separates What-Lies-Beyond and the material realm where we live."

"What?" Suttung cried.

Amalthea said, "It's true. So, after the panic about the discovery died down, the AFA was created on the spot. The news of the discovery of the threat against Earth soon spread at lightspeed among those who worshipped the old religions. Those worshippers then donated money to fund the space program, as it had also been found out that the attack would come from beyond the reach of the magic of Earth. The hereditary witches stepped into the leadership of the AFA to screen every person who wanted to go to the Moon and stop the invasion. They needed to make sure the volunteers were either hereditary witches or were people who had enough natural magical ability. Plus, you know, also have the technical skills needed to make a Moon colony go."

"This is a hell of a way to learn that all of us kids were born some kind of witch," Suttung said.

"Hey, wait a minute. If there're demons, aren't there gods and goddesses and angels and good spirits, too? Why aren't they helping?" Bestla challenged.

"'The Gods help those who help themselves.' That's what my mother says," Amalthea replied.

"What do you mean by that?"

"My mother says that They help us in the exact proportion to the effort that we provide. The more we do, the more They do."

"Were we born to have some kind of destiny or something in stopping the demons?" Suttung broke in.

"No," Deimos said. "We don't have a 'destiny,' but we do have a duty to join in the fight to hold back the demons. That's what the adults have been doing off and on since the demons first started to attempt to break through a year ago. Our parents and the others have managed to beat them off each time, but it's been getting harder lately and the adults need our help."

"This has been going on for a year?" Bestla gasped. Deimos nodded.

"They want us kids to fight demons? We have absolutely no kind of training in doing magic! How can they expect us to help?"

"But we've all been trained, whether you realize it or not, Bestla," Amalthea said. "Think back on all the things we've been doing all our lives: memorizing rituals for god and goddess worship, performing mental meditations in tandem, practicing Tai Chi in groups, and so on. It all had a purpose—to lead us Moon children in learning how to work together and be in sync with each other. Even to having all of our birth names be names of moons in the solar system, we've been groomed from the start to be a community."

"You mean an army," Bestla said sourly.

"Whatever you want to call it," Amalthea said. "The point still is: our parents are out there fighting and need our help."

"Well, all right!" said Suttung. "Let's all get out there

and kick some demon butt!"

"How?" Bestla asked.

Amalthea replied, "The last thing we apparently need to do is realize that everything we've been practicing is real. My mother says we need to remove the last block from our collective sub-conscious."

"In what way are we going to do that?" Suttung asked.

"Let's hold hands and do a quick guided meditation," Deimos suggested. "I suggest the 'Rainbow Stairs' one. But instead of the happy place behind the door once we get to the bottom of the mental steps, how about having the realization that what has been said is true, and that all we need to do is take it into ourselves?"

"Perfect, Deimos!" Amalthea exclaimed.

The twenty-two teens joined hands in a circle and Deimos did the classic 'Rainbow Stairs' meditation fast and smooth. Soon young men and women were dropping their hands from their neighbors' as incredulous wonder flooded through each of them upon opening their individual mental doors.

"It's—it's amazing!" exclaimed a girl. "It's like magic!"

"You mean, it *is* magic," Amalthea corrected her.

"But what, exactly, should we do to help?" Suttung

asked.

"I saw our parents holding back the demons, who looked kind of blobbish, with some kind of light beams. Why don't we envision, I dunno, a giant hand or something?" Deimos replied.

"Yeah! Then we can punch the demons right in the face!" Suttung said with enthusiasm.

"Blobs don't have faces," Deimos grinned.

"You know what I mean!"

A cheer rose from all the others at Suttung's idea.

Amalthea smiled. "Hey, Deimos, if a giant hand punching a demon in the face gets everyone behind the idea, let's do it."

The teens crowded with enthusiasm into the airlock room and cycled through it to exit the station. They went to stand behind their parents and the other adult colonists on the dust of the Moon's surface and looked up. Worryingly, there was no longer just an amorphous blob appearing and disappearing in the perpetual night sky. Now there was what looked like a hole overhead with ugly clawed hands and feet and heads trying to wriggle their way out.

"Eeek!" Bestla's voice shrieked in all the teens' helmets. "There *are* demon faces now!"

"Don't focus on that. Focus on what we're about to do instead!" Deimos' voice replied. "Everybody ready?"

"Ready!" they chorused back.

Deimos led them in another guided meditation to create free-floating energy over their heads as the first step. Some of the teens were able to form energy in a variety of colors, but about half had only empty space above them.

"I can't do it!" yelped a boy, and others took up his panicked cry.

"Try imagining tapping into the colony's power sources!" Amalthea suggested urgently. "Maybe that will help!"

The teens tried again, and this time everyone could feel through the soles of their space boots the thrum of the Moon base step up a couple of notches.

"It's working!" squealed Bestla, as now an eerie blue colored energy manifested over her head which hadn't been there before.

All the other teens who'd had empty space above them also manifested the same blue energy as Bestla. Deimos then guided them all into forming their disparate energies into one huge, multi-colored fist aimed straight at the hole in reality.

"On the count of three, put all your effort into sending our fist flying at the demons! One, two, three!" Deimos said loudly.

The multi-colored energy shot away from the teens and power-housed its way through the adults' magical efforts towards the break in the sky.

"Look!" cried Suttung with excitement.

A crystalline light appeared behind the demons and sped towards them at the same rate as the fist flew at them from in front.

"It has to be from the Gods! They're helping us!" Amalthea shouted excitedly.

The two energies met in a blinding flash of light with the demons squarely between them, like a piece of glass between an anvil and a hammer strike. With a despairing cry that was more felt than heard, the demons shattered. All the colonists, teen and adult alike, started jumping up and down and high fiving each other in celebration as space returned to its normal appearance above the Moon.

Later, over dinner in their apartment, Jane and Richard asked their daughter, "How on Moon were you kids able to pull that off?"

"Well, when we teens accessed our magic, some of

us had problems powering the image. I suggested visualizing tapping into the colony's power sources to help them form their magic. What I *didn't* take into account was that we weren't just doing imagery anymore, but something more. So some of us, like Bestla, actually tapped the atomics instead," Amalthea said.

"So, you mean to say you all gave a nuclear-powered magic face punch to the demons?" her father asked, chuckling. "That's something they're probably going to take a while to recover from."

"It's all very interesting," Jane said thoughtfully. "We'd never thought about using science to back up our magic. You've opened up what promises to be a very interesting field, young lady. Good work."

Amalthea glowed from her mother's praise.

"Yes, indeed," Richard said. "We may have built the technology, but you kids live it. And next time ..."

"Next time, we'll *all* be able to face-punch the demons with magical science!" Amalthea finished with a grin.

Susan Bianculli wears the titles "Mother" and "Wife" most proudly. Another is "Author" for her *The Mist Gate Crossings* series, as well as several short stories in several other anthologies besides this one. To learn about the other things she's had published, check out: susanbianculli.wix.com/home

Weight

Renee Whittington

From beneath a mound of gold coins and baubles accumulated over centuries, the dragon Emarys rose from the pit she slept in to greet the day. Coins spilled down her sides, falling to piles at her feet as she wriggled forward to settle a collar of gold-plated chain mail around her neck. She sighed with relief at its heaviness and donned the rest of her adornments—golden, chain-mail greaves about her hind legs and similar vambraces about her forelegs. She slipped several gold coins into a pocket in one of the vambraces.

Emarys gazed eastward, where the first rays of sunrise would soon peek over the horizon. She trembled with longing and hurried down the corridor separating her sleeping chamber from her day cavern and stretched out supine on her landing ledge.

As the sun rose Emarys crooned at it, lost in its lucent glow. The sight of it dazzled her with its brilliance. Nothing in the universe could be so beautiful, and she twitched with the urge to fly into it, even as the wiser part of herself fought the urge, aided by the metal she wore.

The sun inched above the horizon. Emarys welcomed it with a glad cry and watched as it rose above the trees into the brightening sky. When it cleared the treetops, Emarys launched into the sky, wings spread. It was time for breakfast.

She did not notice the ragged figure hiding in the rocks behind her.

What was I thinking when I decided to climb to the dragon's cave? Merka asked herself.

She clung to an almost sheer wall of stone. Tufts of grass or spring flowers sprouted from cracks in the expanse of gray, but mostly it was just rock. She stood on a narrow shelf of stone that served as a pathway from the city of Chardon below to the cave of its guardian. A wall of stone pressed against Merka's stomach, and nothing but air touched her back.

She resolutely stepped over a muddy patch and fought down her terror of slipping. Not that falling to her death would be much of a loss. What was one less thief to Chardon? But it would be a great loss to her Gran, who was recovering from a heart seizure. Merka squeezed back tears and forced herself onward. It was bad enough leaving Gran with Skinny Meg, who had no more attention than a sparrow.

A day up and back, wait until the dragon left to hunt, steal enough to pay Gorodan back for the loan—plus interest—and get away fast. That was the plan. Emarys was rumored to have a hoard of gold in her cave. Why steal from people who needed their money, when she could steal from a dragon who didn't?

She heard a leathery, *whomping* sound. Merka pressed herself against the rock as an immense shadow cloaked her. She looked up and saw the underside of Emarys' body as she leapt from her ledge. Merka stared with awe. Emarys' scales glittered, and she flew with a grace that any bird must envy.

Merka continued forward until the path expanded into a wide lip of stone that jutted out from a cave entrance. Criss-crossing lines of claw marks showed where Emarys had landed over countless years. Merka looked out at the open air. There was Emarys, flying eastward, so far away that she looked dark. Merka rested on the ledge briefly but soon stood and entered the cave.

The first cavern she came to was nothing but rock and tapestries. Light came from glowing spheres set into the walls. Merka began to wonder if all the stories about Emarys' hoard were just stories. A cushion-topped ledge, suitable for sitting on, curved along one wall. Did the dragon host visitors? She peeked into the small but empty guest bedroom. Apparently, the dragon did.

This is all very fascinating, Merka told herself, *but I need to hurry.* She crossed the tapestry cavern to where the passage narrowed and walked along it until she came to an immense, interior cavern—and stood rooted to the floor.

Gold coins and trinkets lay everywhere, piles of them spilled about, more gold than Merka had ever imagined existed in the entire world. Merka stepped inside onto the hills and valleys of coins. On a whim, she sank to her knees and stretched out on her back, literally lying in the midst of a small lake of gold. As she did so, a gentle breeze seemed to flit over her for a moment before dying away.

How is this possible? Merka wondered. And then outrage sizzled. *Gran and I sleep in filthy alleys every night. I can barely keep us fed and clothed. Everyone I know begs for crumbs that fall from the fingers of the wealthy, yet this dragon, this, this ... creature ... has enough gold in just one of these coins to feed me for a year. Just a few of them could feed all the beggars of Chardon for a life-time—with gold left over! Yet she does nothing with it. How dare she?*

Merka scrambled to her feet and untied the cloth tube from around her waist that served both as her belt and as her carry-bag. She wasn't strong enough to manage sacks of gold, and even the filled tube she tied back around her waist made movement too awkward for her underfed frame. She had to put most of the coins back because the extra weight interfered with her balance. In the end she took only twenty coins from a lake's worth.

But she could pay her debt to Gorodan. She could afford a room for herself and Gran and buy warm winter cloaks. She could even apprentice herself—and not to the Thieves' Guild, either. Relieved, Merka set off back down the mountain.

Emarys was finishing her fifth head of cattle when she felt the warding spell impinge upon her senses.

Someone is taking my gold!

She jerked her head up from her meal and peered toward her cave, eyes narrowed as fear overtook her. This far away, she could see no detail. Emarys shook the coins from her vambrace pocket and let them fall near the carcass she had just eaten; the herdsman would find them. Then she dashed across the field and took off into the air, arrowing toward her cave.

When she finally saw the girl, Emarys could barely credit the sight. *That scrawny child is the thief? She can't have taken much. Still, I won't have children climbing to my cave. If one succeeds, I'll have dozens.*

Hovering in place, Emarys positioned herself in the girl's path and blew a small gout of flame at her. She carefully controlled it, but it got the girl's attention. She yelped, cowered, and slowly moved toward the cave as Emarys directed her.

Sweat poured from Merka's palms as Emarys herded her back into the cave. *I'm dead now. Emarys will kill me!* When Merka reached the ledge she dashed inside the outer cave and waited there, shaking.

The light behind her went dark, and she heard the scrape of claws against rock, the rustling of wings as they were folded close against a body, and the steps of clawed feet.

Turn around ... Merka, a voice said in her mind.

Merka found she could move, even with legs like

jelly. She faced Emarys.

The dragon was the most beautiful yet terrifying creature Merka had ever seen—scales of deep orange along the upper side of her body and wings, with scales of pale gold all below. Her eyes were huge and amber, engulfing her pupils. Around her neck she wore a heavy collar of gold chain mail. A bracelet or anklet of the same encircled each leg.

You do not resemble the usual thieves who come here, Emarys said into her mind as she cocked her head. *Are you here at your own behest or another's?*

Merka bit her lip. "My own," she said. "I owe a debt I can't pay, and I decided to come here."

The dragon blinked. *You accept responsibility for yourself. Refreshing.* Emarys moved deeper into the cave, curling up before Merka's only exit. *And very odd. What persuaded you that my gold was yours for the taking?*

"Nothing—until I saw how much of it you have," Merka admitted. "You could feed all the beggars of Chardon with a handful of this—and all the highborn, too. But it just sits in this cave while the beggars starve. But you don't care. You have no idea how we live."

Ah. And because I have so much more than you, I

am expected to just let you and, I presume, the starveling others, take, and take, and take. Well, I am a dragon. I do not deal that way. I earned every ounce of this gold or was given it as a gift. I have a need for it. Your ignorance of that need does not entitle you to take what is not yours.

"What need could you possibly have?" Merka demanded. "You hunt each morning and spend the rest of the day in here. You don't *do* anything!"

I need not explain myself to a thief, the dragon pointed out, *but I will, because you have asked. I pay the herdsmen in gold for the cattle I eat. I teach. I advise the King, Queen, and their heirs and guard this kingdom from invaders. I am the source of all magic cast in this realm, and I train mages to use it wisely. I need the gold to weight me to the earth. Without it, I would become entranced by the sun, whose creature I am, and fly into it. Every time I fly out to hunt, I take that risk; it is why I wear gold on my person. You cannot know how much of a lure the sun is to me.*

"You have much more gold than you need. As for teaching, you don't teach everybody, only the King's children and mages, I'm betting, only people who can afford to pay you in gold. How often in its entire history has Chardon been invaded? And what do we need magic for that two hands can't do just as well?"

I am teaching you right now and not asking a price, the dragon said dryly. *Magic is better and faster at healing than two hands. A strong enough magical shield can withstand arrows. It takes less time to construct than a stone wall and requires fewer resources. A well-trained mage can cast a patent shield in seconds. A group of them working through me can cast a shield that will last as long as I do.* Emarys rested her head on her fore-claws.

But we digress. The real issue of importance is what is to be done with you. Emarys eyed Merka. *You are no trained mountain-climber. Why are you here? It would have been far easier for you to have stolen money in Chardon and easier for you to have spent your takings there. Why climb to my cave? What debt do you owe, and to whom?*

Merka looked away. "I'm not that great at stealing; I usually have to run lest I get caught. I wanted to find out for myself if the legends of you were true. But mostly, I borrowed money from Gorodan the Money-lender because my Gran needed medicines. I'm late paying. He says he'll hurt Gran if I don't bring him what I owe by the day after tomorrow." Merka grimaced. "I haven't told Gran I borrowed the money.

And I don't really want to steal from you, either, but I can't let Gran be hurt. Gorodan *will* hurt her if I don't bring him what he wants. He's done it before, just to make the point. No one gets between him and money."

Do they not, Emarys replied, her mental tone arid. *Well, you have a problem. I will not allow you to take any more gold from me than you already have. So how are you going to defeat this brute of a moneylender?*

"Defeat him?" Merka stared at the dragon. "You must be insane. Gorodan has a small army of thugs. I'm just me. And—I don't need any more than I already have."

You are not just you, Emarys replied. She regarded the young human who gazed back at her, baffled. *I loathe moneylenders,* Emarys explained. *They are thieves—and you already know what I think of thieves.*

"You'd—help me? Even after I stole from you?" Merka said.

I would help you rid Chardon of an enemy within its borders. That is part of my duty to this kingdom. As payment for your service, I would allow you to keep what you have taken. Emarys paused. *You will have earned it, not stolen it.*

Tears welled up in Merka's eyes, and her voice

shook. "Thank you. I don't deserve it."

Not yet, you don't, Emarys agreed, *but I have faith in you.*

"You can have faith in me if we survive this," Merka replied, frowning. She paused to clear her thoughts. "You can speak into my mind. How many people can you speak to, all at once, if you use the sun? Because here's my idea, if you really want to get rid of Gorodan …"

Merka knocked on Gorodan's front door a day later and waited. The servant who opened the door frowned. "Borrowers go around back," he said.

"I'm here to pay Master Gorodan what I owe him," Merka said with a lowered gaze.

The doorman gave Merka a startled look. He opened the door wider and pointed to a bench in the foyer.

"Sit there," he said. "I'll ask the master."

Merka waited. With satisfying—and alarming— speed, the doorman returned. "The master will see you," he said. The doorman led her to Gorodan's study, admitted her, and shut the door.

Merka shivered as Gorodan the Moneylender peered at her out of his dark, foreign eyes and then bit into one of the two gold coins she gave him. His eyes widened as his teeth sank into the metal, and he fixed her with an even more piercing—and then sly—stare.

"Where did you get this?" he asked.

"Stole it. Where do you think I got it? I followed a couple of highborn ladies out shopping. Had more money than sense. I cut their purses," Merka said.

"Odd. I haven't heard of any noblewomen losing purses in the past week or so … and I would have," Gorodan purred. "Where did you really steal it from, girl?"

Merka rolled her eyes at him. "Do I look stupid? I didn't take the whole purses. I took a couple of coins from each—two for me, and two for you. Those are yours."

"And do you think *I'm* stupid enough to believe any highborn ladies of today walk around carrying coin in their purses that is over two hundred years old?" Gorodan thrust the coin in front of Merka's eyes before snatching it back again. Merka couldn't read the words on the coin, but she could recognize King Madok the Great's hooked nose.

"No, you stole this from somewhere else, girlie, and I want to know where," Gorodan went on. "I have expenses too, you know."

Merka cursed under her breath. *And I should have exchanged the gold for copper before bringing it to him. I'm an idiot. What beggar goes around carrying gold?*

"Do you want the money or not, Gorodan?" Merka shot back. "If you're keeping what I gave you, our business is done."

She yelped with pain as Gorodan snatched her arm and twisted it up behind her back.

"I said, tell me where you got this from, little thief." Gorodan's voice was dangerously soft now, the way it went when he was about to kill someone—or break their fingers or limbs. "Did you break into a bank? A coin collector's house? The counting house of some business? You didn't just take four coins; you'd be a fool to leave so much gold behind. Where's the rest of it?"

"I will never tell you if you don't let go of me!" Merka snarled. She kicked backward at Gorodan's shin, but though he cursed and punched her in the side, he didn't loosen his grip.

"You seem to think I have infinite patience," Gorodan went on. "Where did you steal that coin from? I can make life very difficult—and painful—for your grandmother if you don't tell me."

That frightened her enough to make her tense up, and he punched her again.

Merka gasped from the pain. "Coin collector's house," she blurted. He'd never believe she had climbed the mountain. "Over on—Silverneedle Street."

"You wouldn't be allowed onto Silverneedle Street, dressed as you are," Gorodan said.

"The gods' honest truth, he collects coins—lots of 'em."

"Where? Which house?"

"Third on the right, with the cypress—Agh!" Another punch.

"There are no cypress trees on Silverneedle Street. You've never been there. Shall I cut off an ear, or perhaps a finger, to prove to your grandmother I mean business?"

Bile rose in Merka's throat, and she struggled to swallow it. Her body ached all over, and she feared she would collapse if Gorodan weren't holding her up. "You wouldn't believe me if I told you."

"Try me." Gorodan's words were like shards of ice digging into her.

"I stole it from the dragon. Up the mountain, while she was hunting."

Gorodan slammed Merka against the wall and stared at her. Then he threw back his head and laughed out loud. "By the gods, I should keep you alive just for the entertainment! And what did you find in the dragon's cave, little one?"

Merka sucked in air. "Tapestries, in front," she said. "But in the rear cave, it's nothing but gold—enough to bury yourself in. More than you could count."

"Yet you only brought back four coins. You must think me very credulous, girl."

"I'm not greedy, like you are. And I'm not strong enough to climb down a mountain, carrying a sack of gold on my back," Merka retorted.

"And yet you will go up it again," Gorodan said, "if you want your grandmother to live. And you will bring back far more to me than a mere two gold coins."

Merka froze and then stood trembling. He could break Gran's bones, scald her—and yet, it wouldn't end with her; he still had other customers he would torture if they didn't pay up.

Merka's mouth went dry. "No," she said. "No, I will not. I went there once and got away as fast as I could. I'm not interested in being torn apart by a dragon."

"But apparently you don't mind being cut apart

by *me*," Gorodan said in icy tones. Swift as a snake, he drew a belt knife. "Bad mistake. I shall have to remind you of how things stand between us."

Despite herself, Merka shuddered as she recoiled from him.

He was going to maim the child. Emarys could see it in Gorodan's expression, through Merka's eyes. She could even see it, hazily, in Gorodan's mind, distasteful though it felt to look there. Outrage blazed through her, where she sat upon her ledge, and Emarys let out a great tongue of flame as she drew down sunlight and sent her command.

BRING ME GORODAN THE MONEYLENDER!

Emarys' words thundered through Merka's brain and Gorodan's, as well, almost burning with their fury. Gorodan's tanned face went pale as salt. Outside, Merka could hear exclamations of surprise from house servants and people on the street.

"The dragon knows my name," Gorodan whispered, his eyes huge with shock. He seized Merka by the front of her tunic and pressed his knife against her throat. "What have you done?"

The door to Gorodan's study flew open, and he

yanked the knife away as he glared toward the inter-
ruption. "What?"

"Sir—you're wanted," the doorman said, his face
grim. "Everyone heard it. You've got to leave—now—
before the city guard comes. People are gathering at
the front gate. No one wants to face a dragon's ire."

Gorodan swore. He dragged Merka with him as
he sheathed his knife, yanked open a desk drawer,
and snatched a money purse from it. "Don't just stand
there, fool! Get my horse ready. Tell Hashin to pack
my small chest in the saddlebags. I'll need only enough
food to get to Varda. Move!"

"Hashin's already doing it, sir," the doorman said in
a flat tone. "They're saddling Freshet now."

Gorodan stared at him and then swore again. "Fine.
I'm bringing this girl with me."

The doorman flicked a glance at Merka and then
shook his head. "Riding Freshet double will slow you,
sir. Just get on his back, and go."

"Trying to get rid of me, are you, Tieg?" Gorodan
retorted.

"*Yes.* I'm trying not to burn, sir, and you should be,
too."

"She's my assurance that Emarys won't burn *me*.

So yes, she's coming along. Get moving, girl." Gorodan yanked Merka with him out of his study and out the back door. A tall, bay stallion with lightly-packed saddlebags stood waiting in the stable yard

Gorodan tossed Merka up into the front of the saddle. Merka had never ridden a horse before. With a yelp she flailed one leg over Freshet's back and sat up just as Gorodan squeezed in behind her. Someone—Hashin, Merka presumed—handed him a deep-cowled cloak stitched with runes. Gorodan pulled it on and then held out his hand again. "Bring my sunstone."

Hashin ran back inside the house. He returned and handed a black velvet pouch up to his employer. Merka felt Gorodan stuff it into his jerkin before leaning close to her left ear.

"Give me trouble, and I'll gut you," he said as he took the reins and turned Freshet out of the property's rear entrance. Then they were gone from his residence and out on the streets.

Merka gave Gorodan credit. Though clearly frightened, he kept Freshet to a measured pace and meandered through Chardon's by-ways. The spell-cloak kept him concealed.

But they did not make for the Gate Road. Instead, Gorodan made for an inn built flush against Chardon's city wall. Merka realized that Gorodan owned that inn as well as its mate on the other side of the wall. He had his own secret way in and out of the city.

From there, Gorodan guided Freshet toward the road south to Varda. Once they reached open country-side, Gorodan spurred Freshet into a gallop.

Merka saw the shadow of Emarys' wings upon the road before anything else. Behind her, she felt Gorodan stiffen as the dragon landed in front of them, opened her jaws wide, and bellowed.

Gorodan cursed and fumbled in his jerkin for the sunstone, but Freshet gave him no time for that. The stallion reared in terror at being confronted by such a large, close predator. Gorodan tightened his legs around the stallion's barrel, but it had no effect. Freshet wanted them *off*, and off they went, tumbling to the road as the bay spun on his hind legs and darted away. Gorodan seized Merka and kept her in front of him.

Emarys paced toward them, regarding Gorodan as the two of them scrambled to their feet. *You resemble the royal lineage of Navethia*, she remarked to Gorodan.

The moneylender nodded. "The family disowned my father—I'm sure you remember. If you know that, you know what I have and what I can do with it."

Emarys hissed. *You would so dishonor your family's name and the gift my kind gave to them?* She closed her eyes.

Gorodan shrugged. "They're not my family anymore." He tugged the pouch free of his jerkin and pulled it open, to reveal that the pouch was insulated and contained a fist-sized, glowing, amber-colored crystal that flickered with inner fire and heat.

"What is that?" Merka asked, staring at the gem.

"This is a sunstone," Gorodan replied, his voice all velvet and honey now. He flicked a glance toward Emarys and smiled. "She keeps her eyes closed, but she can't resist it any more than a cat can resist a piece of string—can you, Emarys? You don't have to open your eyes; you can see it through ours, can't you, great one?"

The royal Navethians can command my kind with them, Emarys whispered in Merka's mind.

Instantly, Merka shifted her gaze away from the sunstone, but she could see Emarys digging her claws deep into the road and turning her head away, trembling with the effort to avoid looking at the stone. Merka realized that Gorodan was forcing his vision to her through it.

A great, yawning chasm of *want* filled Emarys, a longing that wracked her body. Emarys opened her eyes and fixed her gaze on the warm, amber sunstone. As simply as that, her turmoil dissolved and was replaced with blazing light that washed everything away, save for a single-minded contentment. Emarys relaxed.

Someone stroked her nose, and Emarys recognized the touch as that of someone Navethian, permitted to approach. *Gorodan.*

"What a beautiful dragon you are. And how beautiful the sun is. You want to be with the sun, don't you, Emarys?"

Oh, yes! Emarys sang to Gorodan and to the girl she still shared a link with.

"Excellent," Gorodan said beside her. "I release you from all cares, Lady Emarys, as I sever your chains now." Gorodan lifted the sunstone and peered into it.

A beam of sunny light shot from the stone and hit the golden collar around Emarys' neck. Merka stared in horror as it melted a line down the chain mail collar, causing it to drip down into a pool at the dragon's feet. Then he did the same with the bracelets and anklets.

"What are you doing? She needs those!" Merka

protested and tried to wrestle the stone from him. Gorodan shook her off.

"Go fly into the sun now, my dear. It's calling you home," Gorodan said as the sunstone's beam faded.

"What?!" Merka spun and stared at Gorodan. "You'll kill her!"

As Merka spoke, Emarys shook her four legs free of the chain mail and spread her wings wide. She took several running steps, and sprang into the air, beating her wings downward to catch more air. Her movements shook the collar off, as well. Then she soared skyward and sunward.

"*NO!*" Merka screamed with voice and mind, with every ounce of love and loss she could put into it. Then she turned to Gorodan and seized hold of the sunstone, yanking it from Gorodan's grasp and peering into it, even though she could feel it burning her fingers. *Emarys, come back to me! PLEASE!*

"You stupid girl!" Gorodan snarled. He drew his knife and stabbed her. Merka gasped as it cut into her side. She bashed the sunstone against Gorodan's head and let it burn him. His head snapped to the side, and he crumpled. Still she held the stone against him as it burned. Merka sagged to the ground alongside him.

Emarys, please don't fly into the sun! Come back! Merka begged before everything went black.

The sun was a universe of light that filled Emarys' soul with magic and warmth. Blinded to everything else, Emarys flew toward it, wings beating the thin air. The sky darkened to indigo as she gained altitude.

Emarys, come back to me, please!

Such a dreadful feeling of loss, Emarys thought distractedly as her flight stuttered for a moment. *How can it penetrate the world of light?* And then her thoughts jangled. *Merka? Merka wants me?*

Looking into Merka's mind was an alien sensation—burning that caused pain, and still more pain that stabbed into Emarys' senses.

He's hurting you! Desire for the sun vanished in the flood of Emarys' alarm. She banked and reversed course, swooping down toward the pair on the Vardan road.

Merka.

Merka tried to shut the voice out, but it was in her head. She couldn't escape it.

Merka. Wake up.

Merka opened her eyes to see a dragon's head lowered over her. She sat bolt upright. "Emarys! You didn't fly into the sun!" Suddenly, Merka was crying, and she reached out to touch the dragon's head.

No, I did not—because you freed me. Emarys' thoughts were filled with awe.

"You freed yourself from the stone," Merka said. "You decided to come back and—you healed me," she said, looking in amazement at her hands, pink with new skin where they should have been scorched black. She glanced about, looking for Gorodan, and saw only a lump huddled under a smoking cloak.

You were willing to fight and die to save me. I was glad to abandon the sun to stop you from being hurt. Emarys lifted her head and gazed calmly at the sun.

Merka's mind overflowed with Emarys' happiness. "Is this what being sun-dazzled feels like?" Merka asked in a subdued tone. "This joy? How could you give it up for me?"

Emarys lowered her head to look at Merka. *Because you are the weight that holds me to the earth now, more powerfully than gold or a sunstone, for we chose each other. Your weight makes me joyous.*

Merka looked at the dragon. "But I won't live forever."

Of course not, Emarys acknowledged, *and that is a concern. But it need not be settled today. We have more immediate concerns.*

Merka blinked at her. "Like what?"

Like what to do with all that gold I no longer need.

By day, **Renee Whittington** orders things like educational items and therapeutic horseback riding lessons for blind children in Houston, Texas. By night, she can be found at Eastern Star meetings and Lighthouse of Houston choir rehearsals. She has been most recently published in the YA science-fiction and fantasy anthology *One Thousand Words for War* and has placed a couple of times in Morgen Bailey's 100-word monthly writing competitions in the past year. Her author blog, *Muse Voices*, is located at: http://musevoices.blogspot.com.

The Witch and the Hunter
Ariane Felix

The Hunter

The trees rise like pillars. They grow from the dirt, their roots and trunks covered in lichen and moss, their leaves blocking the sun. The air clings to my cheek, to the paint on my face. The rifle feels heavy in my hand, sleek. I weave through the trees with slow steps, crushing dead leaves and moist earth. I don't make a sound, but neither does she.

A flock of blue and yellow birds cuts through the sky. I aim my rifle left and right, following the shifting patterns of the forest. She walks through the shadows, in the spaces in between. She's not ethereal, though. A well-aimed bullet will tear through her skin, ribcage, and heart, pierce through each layer of her and carve a hole in her center. I saw her bleed once, and I'll see it again. I'm Hunt, the hunter. It sounds ridiculous, but Hunt is my name and hunting Witches is what I do, what my family has done for ages, ever since the world started the unification.

I lick my lips, tasting water. The forest sweats, and so do I. My tiny brother flanks my back, the rifle's butt sinking into his lean shoulders. I told Kyle to use the smaller gun he carries inside his jacket, but he's just as proud as our mother. Dad died in a hunt before I was born. There are only two of us now. The Witch killed my oldest brother during our last hunt, so now I take the front. I pull my hand up in a fist, a gesture that tells Kyle to stop. My earpiece signals a shift behind the bushes. The gadget drowns out the useless sounds of rivers and bugs and howler monkeys calling to each other. I hear only movement, anything that might potentially be a threat, that might potentially be her.

I swirl two fingers up, and Kyle circles around me, pointing his gun at the trees. I take aim at the bushes. A snake slithers through the moss, a red spiral flashing in my visor. I relax the grip on my rifle. It's an anaconda, its stomach bloated from eating a rodent or a bird. The snake presents no threat to us, but I should get its skin. The species is endangered, but women still need purses. Kyle waits for my command to shot the anaconda with a tranquilizer. But I don't give the order.

"We don't have time to collect," I say as an explanation to my brother. His shoulders deflate. He tries to conceal his pout, conceal the fact that he's a kid. Collecting is his favorite part, but I don't like to kill for nothing. I only like to kill for a reason.

I wipe my thumb over the lenses to clean the condensation. The visor reveals spots of heat. The Witch is made of fire, flames that burn under her fake human flesh. But my visor got cracked last time, and I can only see a messy cluster of red—capybaras and other small critters flashing by, not her. When she registers in the visor, she glows, takes up the whole screen. She looms like a storm cloud, dense and dark, impossible to miss.

We have never come this far into the forest, but the Witch has been taking people, one after the other. Hunting her is necessary. Humankind doesn't need the likes of her. Before, the world had countries, but commerce made those borders thinner, until they became invisible. There are no lands anymore, no demarcations. We forgot about wars. But forests still need to be tamed.

People used to think of Witches as creatures in children's books, but they're real and don't like when we cross their borders. I do the job for the job. The Witches get in the way of bringing resources to the civilized world, so I hunt them. I might be just a guy with a gun, but my work guarantees a world without diseases and hunger. It's important. However, today, I hunt for myself. Because the Witch took my mother.

The Witch

The woman has four fingers now. I chopped off her pinky and squeezed the blood out into the cauldron. I used her snot and the dirt beneath her fingernails and a patch of her skin, too. Smoke rises from the pot and curls around my ears, wraps around my neck. It smells like death and life and all the things in between. It's beautiful. The smoke travels up my nose, and I exhale power.

The potion turns from green to blue, and I take a mouthful. The potion tastes better with each human I add, and this woman has the right kind of blood, full of anger and purpose. I had to wait for two days for her composure to crumble, because I needed her feelings to be ripe. She clutches the bars of her wooden cage and stares at me like I'm a monster. But she's the one who pointed a gun at my forehead, the heat of the laser prickling my skin.

I bang the finger against the edge of the cauldron to get the last drops, but the skin gets scorched and dry. I toss the finger aside. The woman's blue eyes gleam under the firelight. I could scoop them out of her face and watch them melt into my potion. But it's stupid to take a whole eye if a couple of tears will do.

The woman doesn't cower when I approach her. She tips her nose up, and I can see the mucus inside her nostrils, the green dark goo within her.

"They'll come for you," she says. The woman is talking about her two sons, and I'm sure they're in the forest now, stomping onto green leaves with their boots made of dead skin. They're pointing their metal weapons into nothing and hoping to find me because that's what hunters do. The two brothers have been after me since I captured their mother, and they're not even on the right track. If they were close, I would sense their stench. The boys aren't particularly good at their job. Their mother is good; their older brother was good. He is dead now. Such a waste of good blood and tears.

"What is this for?" The woman stares at her finger in the dirt.

I clutch her chin with my shadow fingers, turn her face from side to side until a tear slides down her cheek. I catch it.

The woman should know the answer to that. If I'm here, hidden in a cave made of branches, burning a fire in a forest that quenches flames with its humid breath, it's because of the likes of her.

The Hunter

The Witch leaves a trace, a smell that can be detected by my visor. But nothing shows on the screen. She's far gone. The Witch knows how to hide; the forest is hers, not ours, and that's the problem.

A smile plays at Kyle's lips, his eyes gleaming. He catches a butterfly resting on the trunk of a tree and seals it in a bag. He zips it closed, and the plastic sucks in, freezing the butterfly's blue and bright wings in place. Its beauty has been immortalized. But the butterfly is dead.

Kyle shoves the plastic bag in his backpack. "Should we camp?"

We followed after the remains of her scent for as long as we could, and now we have to rely on the clues she has left on the earth. I scoop up dirt and smudge it across my watch's screen. The software detects traces of the Witch, the screen flashing green. Her shadows leave a chemical behind. Some people think that using equipment in a hunt is cheating. They claim to be able to smell her acrid stench in the moist air. Sometimes,

I believe them. I close my eyes and sense something in the air, beneath the smell of green and water, but I can't name it.

I take off my earpiece, the buzzing of the forest hitting me like a flood. The cicadas fill the air with their song. A river flows nearby. The birds screech and twitter. Everything has a sound. It's too much. But staying with the earpiece for too long causes cancer. Not that I should worry about cancer. Hunters don't have a long life span.

"Hunt?" My brother says over the cacophony of noises.

I think of the Witch's shadow fingers wrapping around my mom's neck, and I don't want to stop to sleep or eat. All of that sounds unimportant. Nobody knows what Witches do, but I heard the stories of dismembered limbs and I have a good imagination. I would walk until my feet dropped, but Mother wouldn't. She always says that you can't catch a Witch if you're dead.

"We camp." The Witch thrives in the night, her shadows dissipate and blend into the forest, making it hard for the sensors in the visor to detect her. She knows that. The Witches have grown smart over the years. If we stay put, the tent will protect us. I pull out the miniaturized tent from my backpack and watch it inflate. The fabric expands, breaking branches and crushing leaves on its way.

The Witch

Humans stink. Their chemicals leave marks on the barks of trees. Their boots smash small plants, and leaves shrivel where they pass. They used to live among us, share the rivers, take the fish that they needed to eat and no more. They worshiped my kind, left offering on the roots of the trees. Now they want to contain the forest in their glass tubes and plastic bags. They want to understand it, and instead they kill it. It's what humans do.

The potion has made me stronger. I don't weave through the trees. I blend. I'm the moist air, the shift in the breeze. The birds fly along with me, the ants trail after my smell because I'm them and they're me. I follow the stench of the brothers, run my shadow fingers through the barks, through the dirt and crushed bugs and fallen leaves.

A thing protrudes amidst the trees, a dark, green mole that tries to blend with the greenery. The two brothers sleep inside this cocoon. I hear their hearts beating in the wind. Their shelter smells like them, acidic and wrong. I slither through the branches of the trees, borrow the eyes of a snake, and see the heat of their bodies—bright, shifting spots of reds and yellows. They don't notice me coming, but their metal objects do.

A screech cuts through the air in waves, makes me recoil my shadow fingers. The green of the foliage blends with the night sky, and now I have legs and hands and can't stretch myself out through the forest. The brothers think they can stop me with their machines, that they can trap me like a butterfly.

They step out of their hiding place with their metal weapons in hand. I open my mouth full of sharp teeth, let them see the darkness inside. They stumble, and I advance. The power sings my body awake. The roar that pours out of my mouth shakes the ground, stirs the birds and bugs, makes the wind howl, and rivers rise. The forest screams for me.

The boys better run.

The Hunter

My vision adjusts, the colors gaining shape. Without my visor, the world looks too sharp and bright, made of curves and textures. Hundreds of sounds invade my ears, and I can't distinguish them because I don't have my earpiece. I force my heart to slow down, my mind to focus.

I'm in a cage made of twisted branches, my back pressed against Kyle's back, our hands tied together. Leaves and dirt and I don't know what else clogs my mouth, and I can't speak or move. My eyes water in anger. The Witch caught us. The alarm should have made her shrink on the dirt like a kid, but instead the Witch screamed and shook the ground and trees and the air itself. I have fought Witches before. I have seen this Witch's shadows dance in the forest, dark clouds of smoke shifting from branch to branch. Her shadows coiled around my oldest brother's ankle and pulled him down; his skull hit a sharp rock hidden in a bed of leaves and cracked open. But she shouldn't have been able to make the forest tremble with the sound of her voice. That's new. Unnatural.

I try to wriggle my hands free and nudge Kyle with my shoulder. His head lolls forward, his weight dragging me sideways. She drugged us. The sharp, tangy taste of herbs lingers on my tongue.

The Witch's shadows flicker past a small fire, but I don't see my mom. My heart constricts, and that's

when the Witch notices me. The shadows gather together, mold into the shape of a face. Her hands move
by themselves, peeling apart something pink and
bloated.

She looks as young as me, her cheeks flushed
red, her hair raven black. But her eyes have no white
parts. They're two bottomless pits. She used to have
normal eyes. I remember her face before she knocked
me down with a branch and took my mom. The Witch
floats toward me, the shadows transforming into arms
and connecting her hands to the rest of her.

I attempt to speak again but almost choke on dirt.
Her sleek fingers probe my mouth, taking out a handful
of leaves. I waste no time and spit on her face. "Where
is my mom?"

She licks my spit, runs her tongue over her lips as if
contemplating the taste. She scoops it up with a finger,
sniffs it, and tosses it in a pot. "You're already ripe."

I shiver. "What's this for?"

Black smoke rises from the fire, flames licking
the bottom of the cauldron. I heard the stories, that
Witches have cauldrons. She stirs its contents. "Your
mother asked the same question."

"Where is she?"

"You are repeating yourself." The Witch's voice moves around me as if being carried by the breeze, and then she yawns, the gesture too human for her.

I fight against the strings holding me, trying to reach for my brother's gun. It's under his jacket. The Witch might have missed it. Branches twist around my wrists as I struggle, the thorns digging into my skin. There's a knife hidden in my left boot, but vines hold my legs in place, and I can't move my hands. I need Kyle to wake up. If we stand, I can shake the knife out of my boot and use it to cut our ties.

"She's in the forest looking for you." The Witch wipes a tear from my cheek, and at first I think she's consoling me. But she walks away from me and watches the tear drop from her finger into the cauldron. "I can see her now. I feel her heart inside my chest. I taste her dry lips."

My vision sways as my heart catches up with my breathing. My mom is alive. Witches don't lie. "How?" I say, but I'm more curious about the why. She should have killed my mother, same as she killed my brother.

"I didn't believe in it at first either." All the shadows merge together, and the Witch sits in front of me, her legs crossed. She has purple bags under her eyes, as if she hasn't slept in days. But Witches don't rest. "She's part of the forest. You're part of the forest, so you're part of me."

"Part of you? So why am I a prisoner?" I scoff. I shouldn't scoff. If the Witch decides I'm too much of a nuisance, I'm dead, and my mom needs me and my brother alive. I can't put his life at risk on behalf of my pride. Not again. If I manage to not spew the first thoughts that come to my mind, maybe I can convince her to release me and my brother like she released my mother. The Witch can keep my snot and tears and whatever else she wants, as long as I get to save Kyle and see my mom again. "If you let us go, we'll leave the forest. We—"

"More will come." She twirls her hands in dismissal. "And I need you."

"For what?"

She cocks her head to the side, and if not for her pitch-black eyes, she would look like a girl. "To kill you."

My breath catches in my throat, but I recover. I even put on a smile. "I thought I was part of you. If you kill me, aren't you killing yourself?"

She stands up at once, dark smoke trailing after her. If I didn't know better, I would say she looks tired.

"How many people have you taken?"

"Enough." She feeds the fire with more wood. "No more than enough."

"And how much is enough?" Rage itches the tip of my tongue. "Did my brother serve his purpose?"

"Your brother died too soon, which is a shame. I needed him alive to gather his blood and tears."

She talks about my brother dying like it was an accident, like she wasn't the one who murdered him. "He has a name. We all have names, unlike you."

"You don't use his name. You call him brother." She smiles like a normal girl would smile, a hint of mockery in the curve of her lips. "You two used to fight all the time, your raised voices like spiders crawling in my ears."

"Why are you talking to me?" It's the wrong thing to ask. The question gives me no upper hand. That's why my oldest brother was the leader and not me. We did fight all the time, and he was always right. If I hadn't tried to chase after the Witch at night by myself, he would still be alive.

"I don't know," she says after I have given up on an answer.

My jaw tightens. "Are you going to kill Kyle, too?"

Again, it's the wrong thing to ask. If she hasn't considered killing him, she sure is thinking about it now. Mother always says that my mouth and heart are connected, and she doesn't mean that in a good way. My emotions cloud my judgment. "He's a good boy. He's innocent."

"Innocent? No human is innocent." She turns to me, and her eyes have never been so dark. Smoke drifts around her. "I'll kill all humans."

The Witch

I find myself in a bed of leaves, ants crawling on my face. My head feels light; a softness spreads through my body. I rub my eyes for no reason and want to lie down again, stretch my arms, and forget. What is this? I have seen humans huddle together like bees do in the winter, but I never had to lie down and sleep. I'm like the air; the air needs no rest.

The fire recedes into the charred tinder, and I sprint to the cauldron to tend the flames. The potion almost dried out. I scrape the bottom and lick under my fingernails. Power courses through me, so much of it, I crumble to my knees. The boy's tears mixed well with his mother's tears. But the brothers are gone, their cage ripped open. If I wasn't so drowsy from sleep, I would have noticed that sooner. I'm a Witch, not a human, and my eyes should always be open.

The potion changed me in more ways than one, but I have no time to dwell on it. The brothers are the key. They come from a generation of Hunters; their blood is stronger than I thought. It's the right kind, and I need all of it.

How dare them? They took advantage of a moment of weakness to scurry away like rodents. That's what humans do. Now the brothers are running toward their base to warn the others about me, and the humans will crowd the forest armed with hundreds of metal weapons and their unnatural chemicals. They'll want to trap me in metal bars and rip me into parts, as they have done to many of my sisters. The other Witches have passed on their blood to me, and today I honor their deaths.

The humans will never catch me. I'm the howling wind. I'm the storm, and they'll all die before they can take another breath. I stretch my shadows, run them thin and far, merging myself into the breeze. The leaves tremble as the wind tears through the trees. They crash, catching in flames, because I'm made of fire, and my anger burns.

I find the brothers easily, two dark spots in the greenery. I'm everywhere, and humans will never be able to hide from me again. The clouds condense in the sky in dark swirling shapes. I descend on the ground, the scorched grass and trees bending with the force of my presence. The brothers run and stumble on their feet. Rain pours over us.

I walk slowly. I have no rush. They're mine.

The younger boy disappears under broken trees, but the older one stops. He turns to me, his fists clenched, his hair like dark water running down his cheeks. "You take me. Let Kyle go."

"Humans never ask for permission, do they?" My voice echoes in the rain. "So don't you tell me what I can take."

"Please." His lips tremble, either from cold or fear.

"You want my pity?"

"I want to save my brother." He raises his hands up and kneels to the ground. "He's young and innocent."

"Your *innocent* brother has a collection of bugs. I saw him dissecting a bird once. You think I haven't seen him in action?" I let my shadow fingers travel to him, cast him in darkness. "Humans destroy everything."

"We do?" His lips curl in a grimace. "Look around you, Witch."

Maybe it's the spite in his voice that brings me back to myself, or maybe it's the truth in his words that makes me stop. I collect my shadows, and the clouds clear.

Trees lie at my feet as far as the eye can see, smoke rising from their dead, charred corpses. Because I set fire to the forest with my anger, and then I doused it in water. Hot tears brim at the corners of my eyes, and that's when I feel the heat in my center. Dark blood spills out of a hole in my stomach, a wound that could only be caused by a human weapon.

It makes no difference. I'm already dead inside. I killed the forest, and the forest is me.

The younger boy called Kyle, the innocent one, creeps out of the shadows of the fallen trees. He drops a metal weapon to the ground. It falls without a sound.

We all do.

Ariane Felix was born and raised in Brazil. She left her job in computer science and moved to Texas in 2011 to pursue a career as a writer. She spent her childhood rummaging through her brother's closet—where she thought books came from—and now writes middle grade and young adult novels that bend toward the weird and the creepy.

Loyalty and Honor
Valerie Hunter

As soon as Corliss stepped onto the green, she knew something was afoot. Talking was prohibited, but glances and eyebrow waggles were exchanged at rapid rates.

Clearly it hadn't been the day to skip breakfast, but how could she have known? Besides, extra sword practice was time better spent. She'd find out the news soon enough.

Corliss glanced at Ezry beside her, but he didn't look at her. Usually he joined her early morning sword practice, but he hadn't today. She was getting worried. The closer they got to Second Year, the more distracted he seemed.

Kerwin strode across the green, and everyone stood straighter.

"As many of you know, a dragon flew over the kingdom last night for the first time in two years." Kerwin's words boomed straight into Corliss. "Before the next full moon, I mean to train you in the ways of bleeding a dragon."

Corliss grinned. This was how she would get herself on the top of the Second Year list, prove herself worthy of being a knight.

Kerwin lectured on dragons, and Corliss did her best to memorize every word. Some of it she already knew. Dragons only came out at a full moon. Their blood could cure almost anything, but it had to be taken from a living dragon.

She learned some things, too. A dragon's fire was hotter than any forge, its teeth sharper than a sword. Bringing it down required enough arrows to ground it but not kill it, and then a brave squire to approach the downed dragon and bash it on just the right place on the skull to knock it unconscious before its exsanguination.

Corliss pictured it. She had a little trouble imagining the dragon since she'd only seen drawings, but she could easily see herself doing the bashing and the draining, being a hero.

Kerwin ended his speech with, "It takes a special squire to put down a dragon. One who is skilled and brave, patient and smart. One who truly embodies the knight's code. I wish you all the best of fortune."

The squires trooped off the green and then immediately began buzzing. Corliss turned to Ezry. "It flew over the boys' barrack? Did you see it?"

He shook his head, looking miserable and exhausted.

Someone nudged between them. "Lucky you didn't get killed out there, Ez," Wati said in a way that implied he wouldn't have cared if Ezry had. "If we need bait for this hunt, we know who to use."

Wati kept walking. Corliss turned to Ezry. "What's he talking about?"

"Later," Ezry said, jaw tight.

They had aerial target practice with Kerwin. Corliss and the other squires had used the bows before, but at stationary targets or a heavily armored knight charging toward them. This time, to practice what it would be like to shoot a flying dragon, Kerwin had a man throw fowl from the high tower.

Corliss had been passable at the previous archery lessons, but hitting the birds seemed impossible. Fortunately, not many of the other squires did better, so she didn't feel like a complete failure. Besides, they had nearly a month to practice.

The day passed without an opportunity to talk to Ezry. She couldn't find him at dinner, so she sat with Adira instead. She and Adira had grown up at the same orphanage, had been the only two to have been accepted into the kingdom a year ago, she as a squire and Adira as a physician's apprentice.

Corliss told Adira all about the dragon, but the longer she talked, the deeper Adira frowned, until finally Corliss was forced to ask, "What?"

"Dragons, dragons, dragons. You sound like Abba. Remember her? Working herself into a tizzy whenever she saw a horse?"

It was Corliss's turn to frown. Abba had been all but simple. "I am *not*—"

"You're worse! A horse was never going to kill Abba."

"I'm not getting myself killed!"

"I had to copy over the castle death registry for the past decade. Do you know how many squires were killed by dragons in that time? Thirty-seven. And I bet every one of them didn't expect to get killed."

Corliss didn't think that was a terribly large number, but she didn't say so. Instead she said, "It's my job."

"Maybe. But you don't have to sound so excited about it,"

Corliss didn't respond. Adira just didn't understand.

It was evening before Corliss finally got Ezry alone. "What's wrong?"

"I haven't been sleeping well. And then last night ..."

"What happened?" she asked when he didn't go on.

"I had a nightmare, and I woke up outside."

"Outside the barrack?"

"Outside the castle wall! The guard found me at dawn, after he'd lost the dragon."

She tried not to dwell on the embarrassment of that, or the fear. "I didn't know you sleepwalked."

"I don't! Never before, anyway."

"What did you dream about?"

Ezry looked away. "I think it was the dragon."

"Maybe it wasn't a dream. Maybe you really saw him." It made her feel shivery inside to think of Ezry half asleep and defenseless seeing the dragon.

"I don't think so. I've had the same dream for weeks, it was just worse last night. And I don't actually see the dragon. I just ... know it's there. It's like I'm flying with it."

"Oh." That didn't sound particularly frightening to Corliss, but then again she wasn't the one who'd woken up outside the castle wall.

"Every time I wake up from one of those dreams, I'm scared," he said.

She shook her head as though it might clear his words from her ears. They'd agreed that they'd be knights no matter what. Knights weren't afraid.

"It'll be all right," she said, cutting him off before he could say anything else. "We'll kill the dragon, you and me. We'll be heroes."

Ezry didn't answer, but she pretended not to notice.

Every day after that, their training revolved around the dragon. In addition to the aerial archery, they practiced bludgeoning melons, pretending they were a dragon's head. There was a knack to it—hard enough to dent the rind but not to break it. Most of the squires couldn't perfect it, but Corliss was good at it, and so was Ezry.

They trained late in the evening, too, in darkness, so they'd be ready. Sometimes Corliss could barely contain her excitement, but Ezry continued to be morose.

"You still having trouble sleeping?" she finally asked him.

He shrugged, which she knew meant yes.

"Maybe you should visit Adira. She could give you a sleeping draught."

"I don't want to sleep more," he said. "When I sleep, I dream, and the dreams—"

"Don't say they scare you!" she interjected. She could hear a harshness in her voice that she hadn't quite meant to be there, but she didn't apologize. "Don't you remember how we swore we'd be better than all of them?"

Ezry was an orphan like her, though he'd come from a different orphanage. All the other squires were the children of knights or minor nobles in the kingdom. They had been pages since they were small and seemed to know everything. They had wanted nothing to do with Corliss and Ezry, so the two kept getting thrown together. Soon enough Corliss had realized that Ezry might be a little quieter and clumsier than she was, but he had the same fire within, the same doggedness. They were going to be knights no matter what anyone else thought of them, and there was no room for fear.

"The Second Year list is in two weeks," she reminded him. "We're going to be at the top. That's all that matters."

"Is it?" he asked.

She grabbed his arm. "You know it is," she said, and walked off before he could say anything else that would make her feel like she didn't know him.

The day before the full moon, Kerwin called them to the green and assigned squads for the dragon patrol.

Ezry wasn't next to her. Corliss hadn't seen him all day. Maybe he'd finally gone to see a physician. He'd have to be better tomorrow, though. He couldn't miss the dragon patrol.

Kerwin called her name as a bludgeoner and drainer, with Rayla and Wati as her archers. They were assigned to the eastern woods. Corliss tried not to think of having to share her glory with Rayla and Wati, neither of whom she particularly liked. They were good archers; that was all that mattered.

She didn't hear Ezry's name. Was he that sick?

After they'd been dismissed, she caught up with Amil, one of the least annoying squires. "Where's Ezry?"

Wati shouldered in. "You didn't hear? Your Ez deserted. Disappeared over night, the coward."

Panic spread through Corliss. "He must've sleep-walked again. He could be hurt somewhere—"

"Not unless he sleep-packed all his things and sleep-made his bed."

She wanted to deny it, to stick up for Ezry the way she always did. But there was nothing to say. He'd left, and he hadn't even told her.

She shut away her thoughts. She could do that, almost. That was the focus it took to be a knight. To have an awful day, to be betrayed by your closest friend, and to keep going and pretend nothing had happened.

That evening Adira found her outside the barracks. "For you," she said, holding out a small contraption with sharp teeth and a long tail of tubing. "I got it from the head physician. He uses it for draining blood-fever patients, but it should work on a dragon. Maximum efficiency. That is if the dragon doesn't kill you first."

"Thanks," Corliss said, ignoring the part about possibly being killed.

"Did you know there's a school of thought about where dragons go between full moons?"

Corliss had no idea what Adira was talking about, but she couldn't bring herself to say so.

Adira told her anyway. "It's thought that dragons are just regular people, and the moon transforms them."

"That's the most ridiculous thing I've ever heard!"

"I found two books about it, including one by a man who saw it himself. He wrote all about a dragon-woman he knew."

"Fairy tales," Corliss said. "Why are you reading about dragons, anyway?"

"I read when I'm worried. Sometimes knowing things eases my mind." She paused. "It didn't this time."

"You don't have to worry about me."

"No? Because someone should. You want to talk about fairy tales? You're the one who seems to want to live in one."

"I don't—"

"Do you know how many squires actually become knights? It's a very small number."

"I *know* that. I'm not an idiot."

"No, but sometimes you need to open your eyes. You act like all it takes is some bravery and skill, and you'll be all right. And sure, that's something. But it takes luck, too, and when have we ever been lucky, Cor?"

Corliss clenched her jaw. "Luck got us here, didn't it? We could have been maids or worse, like all the rest."

"But we're still expendable, just like we were at the orphanage. It's the same for me as you. Half the apprentice physicians fail in the first year, and I know I won't do that. But the rest get sent to work in the fever wards, and most of them die of the fever themselves. Just like all those squires getting killed by dragons—"

"It's called life, Adira! Sometimes people die! At least we've lived first!"

Adira shook her head. "We're just the kingdom's puppets, and you can't even see it. You're just blindly loyal—"

"I can see just fine. I can see you're a white-livered craven! Leave the kingdom if you want. As for me, I don't need luck, and I'm not a puppet. I'm doing what I've always wanted to do."

Adira stared at her, and Corliss wanted to apologize, to tell her they were really meant for Ezry, who wasn't here to yell at. Instead she marched off and didn't look back.

The entire next day felt wrong. Corliss wasn't scared, but she didn't feel like herself. When evening came, she was the last one in the courtyard. It was her job to drive the wagon with its load of bottles. She imagined all of them full of dragon's blood, herself triumphant.

She followed Rayla and Wati, who were on horseback. They rode to the edge of the forest, the full moon producing an eerie light. Rayla and Wati took their positions in the blind they'd already made. Corliss left the wagon at the forest's edge and crouched, looking at the sky.

Time crawled. Corliss stayed somewhere between rest and alertness, ready to spring to action but in the meantime nearly sleeping.

And then a crash, so close it lunged into her ears. She reached for her sword, and was shocked that it was actually firm beneath her fingers.

This was not a dream.

Something was in the air above her.

Corliss couldn't breathe for staring at it, had never seen anything as glorious, as magnificent, as that dragon in flight, silhouetted against the moonlit sky.

When the arrows hit, she bit her lip to keep from yelping. She had forgotten about Rayla and Wati, forgotten her own task. She let go of the sword and felt for Adira's contraption in her cloak pocket, then collected jars and her bludgeon, all the while watching the dragon.

It had been hit, but it didn't fall. The arrows rained on it, and it twisted, jolted, staggered, still aloft, bellowing now, first just a noise, anguished and indignant, and then a stream of flames that made Corliss flinch even though it was nowhere near her.

She heard another scream, human this time. Wati? Corliss squinted through darkness and chaos as the dragon let one more breath of fire go in the direction of the blind before hurtling to the ground, thrashing and writhing against the dirt.

Rayla and Wati had done their job. Corliss could hear Wati's muffled cries retreating as Rayla dragged him away. It was up to her now.

She stood still for a long moment even as her mind screamed at her to move, to drain that dragon dry before it died. Little puffs of flames came out of its mouth with each tortured breath, and her stomach burned with the fear of it.

She moved, finally, because she was a squire, and this was her job. She wasn't going to be some wash-up, some coward.

She approached it from behind, bludgeon tight in her hand. The dragon had seemed so large in the air, but on the ground she could see its body was hardly bigger than her own, though its tail nearly doubled its length. Its wings were impressive in span but delicate; she could see the moonlight through them in a way that reminded her of the stained glass in the cathedral windows.

She counted three arrows, one in its wing and two in its back, all of them quivering as the dragon continued to thump around. Was it her imagination, or were its movements getting weaker? Maybe it wouldn't be so hard to give it a quick hit to the skull ....

Just that quickly, the dragon reared, nearly hitting her with its wings as it bellowed fire into the sky. Corliss tried to retreat, but there was nowhere to go; the dragon was enormous again, a whirlwind of wings and tail and noise, and she was going to die, going to—

Silence.

Pitch dark.

She opened her eyes to find the dragon at her feet, as though this last demonstration had spent all its energy. She raised the bludgeon, but a dragon wasn't a melon. Suppose she killed it or it killed her or—

She jabbed the contraption into the dragon's back, trying to stay well away from its head. It twitched, and she got ready to flee but continued to stand there, holding the siphon and the jar steady with one hand, still clutching the bludgeon in the other. She was being a fool, she needed to knock it out, needed to—

The dragon turned and she raised the bludgeon, trying to reposition herself to get at the base of its neck, trying to get out of range of any flames. The angle really was impossible.

The dragon looked right at her. She shifted again, but it didn't do anything.

The first jar was spilling over with blood, and Corliss forgot about the bludgeon for a moment as she switched jars. The dragon was barely moving now, just the heaving of its sides as it breathed and the slight twitch of its head as it seemed to follow her with its eyes in a way that she found unnerving.

No, more than unnerving.

Familiar.

She knew those eyes.

She knew those—

The impossibility of it crashed into the certainty of it and hit her in a wave of fear so cold she shook all over.

The dragon had Ezry's eyes.

She lunged, pulling the contraption out as the second jar filled, and then staring in horror at the blood continuing to pour out of its—*his*—back. She ripped off her cloak and pressed it against the wound. How could he—why hadn't he—

She locked her eyes on his, the only part of him she

knew.

"I'll get help," she said, her voice coming from somewhere far away, a place where things seemed less impossible.

In the past year, Corliss had done many difficult things, but nothing had been harder than standing in front of Kerwin and giving her report.

"It got away," she repeated, trying to achieve the perfect tone for this complicated lie.

"We'll send a patrol," Kerwin said. "It must be weak."

"It didn't look weak," she insisted. "I doubt we'll see it before the next full moon."

"Still, we'll search at first light. Which direction did it fly?"

"Southwest," she said, putting all the certainty she could into the word.

Kerwin nodded, then put a hand on her shoulder. "This jar is the first dragon's blood we've gotten in four years. You did a fine job tonight."

Just a few hours ago his words would have sent her soaring, but now they were meaningless. "Thank you, sir."

He gave her a nod and sent her to bed, and she went

so as not to rouse suspicion. She didn't sleep, could hardly hold herself together during breakfast. Kerwin organized a patrol of the southwest woods, and she volunteered because it was the only thing she could think to do. It wasn't until midday that she got away, forcing herself to walk even though her legs itched to run, trying to empty her mind with every step and failing. What if Adira hadn't gotten there in time? What if he'd killed Adira, or—

Ezry wasn't where she'd left him, but before she could panic Adira motioned to her from the forest's edge. Her face was a mask of all the fear and worry Corliss could feel clawing at her own stomach.

"I dragged him in here," Adira said, voice low but still panicked.

Corliss could see him now, just a boy covered by her cloak. He looked so tiny. "Is he ..."

"He's not good. He changed at sunrise. It was ..." Adira shook her head. "I did what I could, but he needs a physician."

"We could take him back," she suggested, even though she knew they couldn't. "He's not a dragon anymore; we could—"

"What? He's got three arrow wounds! They'll figure

it out, they'll ...."

Adira didn't finish, but Corliss could well imagine what they'd do. Kill him. Or cage him, wait for the next full moon, and then drain him dry.

Like she had tried to do.

Something was breaking within her, and she clenched it back together. "We need to get him somewhere safe."

Adira nodded. "There's a cave up ahead. The two of us should be able to carry him."

They managed. "Has he been awake at all?" Corliss asked.

"A little, when I first got here. When he was still a dragon. I was ...."

"What?" Corliss prompted.

"Scared. I was scared. I didn't go to him till he passed out."

"It's all right," Corliss said.

Adira shook her head. "He lost a lot of blood. The arrows weren't lodged deep, but the other wound..."

The wound she had made. "Did you use the blood I gave you?"

Adira nodded. "But I'm not sure dragon's blood works miracles on a dragon."

"He's not a dragon *now*."

"No."

Corliss looked at Ezry's still form. They had laid him on his belly, and Adira had pulled back the cloak so Corliss could see all the bandages on his shoulder and back. All the blood.

"He could have told me," she said, letting anger rise within her. Anything to dull the fear. "He *should* have told me."

"The book I read, about the dragon woman? It said she didn't know. When she was a woman, she didn't remember being a dragon."

"But all this time ...."

"I think this was just the second time he changed. The book said it doesn't happen till a person reaches maturity."

So he hadn't known. Of course he hadn't known. He would have told her. Her certainty over that only made her feel sadder.

They sat there for a long time. Ezry didn't move. Corliss didn't move. Every now and then Adira checked Ezry's bandages, but that was all.

Finally Adira said, "You need to go fetch me some more bandages and blankets and herbs. Food, too."

"You go," Corliss said.

"You're sneakier. I'll tell you where everything is."

The next few days were a blur of fear and subterfuge. Corliss did what she needed to do as a squire, and then sneaked back to the cave at night with supplies. The dragon's blood seemed to be working, or so Adira claimed.

On the third night, Adira met her outside the cave. "He's awake."

Joy spread within Corliss. "Good."

"Go see him."

She nodded but didn't move, changing the subject instead. "Don't you need to go back?" She wasn't sure if physician apprentices were kept track of as closely as squires. "Your first year test must be soon."

Adira looked away. "It was two days ago."

Her words hit Corliss in the gut. "You should have …."

"What? Said, 'Sorry, I can't save Ezry's life, I have a test to take?'"

"Maybe they'd let you take it later?"

"You know that's not how it works."

Corliss tried to find something to make it right, but she already knew there was nothing.

"Stop looking like my life has ended," Adira said. "I

don't obsess over my future in the kingdom like you do. Sometimes I'm more than happy to let fate intervene. Or at least happy enough to avoid the fever wards."

"Where will you go?"

Adira shrugged. "I'll stay here as long as Ezry needs me. Then ... well, there are other kingdoms. Or perhaps there's a village that could use a half-trained physician."

"They'd be lucky to get you," Corliss murmured. The words seemed inadequate.

Adira shrugged. "Go see Ezry."

Inside the cave, Ezry was sitting up, pale in the lantern light but definitely alive. Before she could say anything, he said, "Thank you."

She stared at him. "Why are you thanking me? I nearly killed you."

"Adira says you saved my life."

"*She* saved your life."

"But you're the one who sneaked back and fetched her. You're the one who gave her the blood to use."

She shook her head, words sticking in her throat.

Ezry said, "I'm sorry. For leaving and not telling you."

He sounded like he was having trouble talking, too. At least he had said something. She should be the one apologizing. She should—

"Did I ever tell you how I came to the orphanage?" Ezry asked, not quite looking at her.

"You were a baby," she said. Why was he changing the subject?

"Yes." He didn't say anything else for a long moment, but Corliss could feel the words crowding in, and at last they spilled over. "I was found in a cave. By Kerwin."

Corliss tried to fit these facts together. "Kerwin?"

"He was hunting a dragon, him and his mates. They killed it, and then they found me. They figured the dragon must've killed my mother."

The words sank into Corliss like talons.

"Kerwin said it was a nice little home in that cave. My mother's things neat and clean, and a cradle .... I thought that's why I was having the dreams, about the dragon that killed my mother. That's why I left, to see if I could find that cave. Finally get over that fear. I didn't want to tell you because I knew you'd talk me out of going."

She nodded. She would have tried.

"But now I know the dragon didn't kill my mother." He sounded desperate for her to catch on.

She did. "The dragon was your mother."

He nodded, eyes clouded over with tears. "I really did want to be a knight. I thought I could be a good one, too, even if I didn't have your skills, your confidence. But after those dreams … I knew I couldn't be. I was too scared. And then it turned out I'm a monster."

"You're not."

"I could've killed you!"

"You didn't." She paused. "You kept looking at me. I think you knew me."

He shut his eyes. "I don't remember."

She wanted to tell him that was good. She didn't want him to remember the pain she'd inflicted. She wanted to tell him she still knew him, no matter what he was. She wanted to say so much.

"You'll be a good knight," he said. "You were meant for that. There's nothing I wanted more than to be side by side with you, but … let's say good-bye now."

"What?"

"You might get caught if you keep sneaking out here. And I have to leave as soon as I'm able. I have to be long gone by the next full moon." He shoved something into her hand, a tiny vial of red. "In case you ever need it, when you're a knight."

"Thanks," she whispered.

He nodded, then turned his head away. She left without saying anything else to him or Adira. She didn't know how to say good-bye.

The following evening Corliss stood in her place on the green, except it didn't feel like her place without Ezry next to her. She'd imagined the Second Year list a thousand times and with multiple outcomes, but all of those scenarios included Ezry.

Kerwin was speaking, but for the first time Corliss didn't fully listen until he started reading the names, from the bottom of the list to the top. Shoulders began to sag while others grew tenser, expectant. And then the list was over and hers was the last name, the one left ringing in everyone's ears.

"You are one year closer to being knights," Kerwin said. "To taking the oath to the kingdom you love above all, to pledging your loyalty and honor."

The words hit her in the heart. She thought of Adira going into the woods without question when she'd asked her to, of Ezry thanking her and giving her the vial of his blood. Everything she thought she knew seemed to be sliding beneath her feet.

"Tomorrow, your first task as second year squires

will be a patrol of the eastern forest. I mean to discover where the dragon's hiding so we'll know exactly where to look next full moon. Or you might catch it napping and take care of it tomorrow. Dismissed."

They trooped off the green and then dissolved, celebrating and sobbing. Corliss didn't listen to any of it. Even if she went now to warn them, Ezry was still too weak to get far with just Adira to help him—

Rayla tugged on the arm. "I'll help you drain the dragon this time. It's not getting away again. Not after what it did to Wati."

"How is he?" Corliss asked, distracted.

"Still with the physicians. They think his arm's crippled for good."

"Can't they use dragon's blood on it?"

Rayla snorted. "They're not wasting dragon's blood on a squire." Her expression was so fierce and sad that Corliss realized Wati was her Ezry.

You had to be fierce for the people you loved. You had to protect them.

Corliss went back to the barrack, found everything she needed, and arranged her bed to make it look like someone was sleeping in it. She'd done it before. No one had ever noticed or cared.

She walked to the physician's ward, trying not to think about the precious minutes she was wasting. Wati looked surprised to see her. "I suppose you made first name?"

She nodded.

"You deserve it," he said in his grudging way.

She knew better than to thank him. She fingered the vial in her pocket, thinking of all the awful things Wati had done and said to her and Ezry over the past year. Besides, what if he told, sounded the alarm—

Wati's voice interrupted her thoughts. For once it wasn't grudging or sarcastic; it was just sad. "I would've been a good knight."

"Maybe you still can be," she said, shoving the vial into his hand. Because he might be awful, but he wasn't a snitch. And he would make a good knight.

"What's this?" he asked, but she could tell he already knew.

"Use it," she whispered. She didn't need it. The forest was waiting, and Ezry and Adira. If she went, too, they could get him safely away.

That was where her loyalty and honor belonged. That was where she wanted to be.

Valerie Hunter is a high school English teacher as well as a graduate student at Vermont College of Fine Arts' Writing for Children and Young Adults program. Her short stories have appeared in anthologies including *Real Girls Don't Rust, Cleavage: Real Fiction for Real Girls, One Thousand Words for War, Brave New Girls,* and *(Re)Sisters.*

What Hands Cannot Hold
J.G. Formato

Nothing tangible was ever placed in her cauldron, the Wood-Witch explained. Only charlatans and amateurs brew potions with herbs and newts. Magic is intangible, as is its creation.

A sunbeam, distorted by the dirt of the window pane, bent and crashed into the recesses of her pot. Its small light undulated in the curve of darkness, waiting. Her hands, lined with age and scars, grasped a coolness in the air. She wrestled a curious wayward ghost, trapping it in those powerful hands and bending it over her vessel until it exhaled. The shade's breath mixed with the sunbeam's glow, and a steady steam began to rise.

Iris didn't see the sunbeam, nor was she aware of the spirit. She saw a wave of hands, a flash of black eyes, and a toss of tangled grey hair. A timid vapor crept out of the cauldron and settled over its wide mouth, awaiting instruction.

"You are certain?" the Wood-Witch asked.

"I left with nothing. I have nothing but myself to

give. I am certain." Iris's journey was defined by certainty, by the conviction that she would never return to her home.

The witch smiled, she had the final ingredient—consent.

Old hands grasped young ones, twisting the white palms upright. In her mind's eye, the witch threaded a binding needle. A golden thread, corded with strands of magic, commitment, and debt slipped easily through its waiting eye. Iris didn't see the needle, but she felt the pricks and punctures as the witch did her work, stitching their hands together with an invisible thread until she was fully bound. Half in mumble, half in song, the old woman recited her spell.

> *"Your hands are mine, you work for me*
> *Your days are mine, you shall not flee."*

"364 of my days are yours," Iris reminded her. She didn't need a spell to make her keep her word. The promise of that one day was enough.

"That's right. 364 are mine. 1 is yours, from sun-up to sundown. Which day do you choose? Tomorrow, I suppose?"

Iris was surprised. She hadn't expected the witch to be so forthcoming with her part of the exchange. Her heart swelled, crushing the air from her lungs, and she opened her mouth for a joyful yes.

The wind howled at the window, battering the panes and fighting for entry. The smudged glass had darkened as the sun slipped away, deserting the land to escape the frigid gusts. The days were so short now. Iris contemplated the darkness.

"No. I'll wait," she decided. "I choose the longest day. I choose the Summer Solstice."

The Wood-Witch shrugged. "Suit yourself, Princess." But when she turned to stoke the fire, Iris swore she heard her mumble something about brains over ball gowns.

"What did you say?"

"I said, that cauldron is not going to clean itself." A scrub brush sailed through the air and pegged Iris squarely in the chest.

Iris worked faithfully, from dawn to dusk, each and every day. The Wood-Witch was a demanding, but not a cruel, mistress. Iris swept and mopped, cooked and carried. She fed the familiars and tended the herb garden. She led love-struck girls, childless wives, and anxious mothers through the wooded maze of the forest to the creaking, shadowed hut. She handled the payment, so that the witch's hands would not be sullied with such 'uncouth and earthly' matters, leaving her free to pour herself into her art.

Iris became the witch's hands as her own changed. Blisters raised, erupted, and fell until a range of callouses dotted Iris's previously unmarred skin. Skin that had never seen a day's work or toil, not until she had begged the Wood-Witch to take her.

The nights were hers. To rest or to dream—mostly to dream. And the nights were getting shorter.

She woke the Wood-Witch just before dawn. At sunrise, the Solstice would begin, and she would not lose one precious moment. Gripping the leathered skin, she whispered,

"Your hands are mine, you work for me
This day is mine, you shall not flee."

The day broke, golden rays shooting like arrows through the pristine glass. Cunning black eyes opened and twinkled in the rising sun. "And what would you have me do?"

"What you promised. I want to be with him."

"As you wish, Princess." The witch rose and strode to the cauldron with a vigor she rarely showed her customers. Nothing tangible went into the cauldron: a sigh on the wind, a beat of the young girl's heart, a cry of longing that rose from the Underworld.

Swirling mist rose confidently from the cauldron and enveloped Iris, caressing her skin and drawing her outside with insistent fingers. The door slammed behind her, and a violent click of the lock echoed throughout the forest.

Iris shook with rage. The Wood-Witch had tricked her, stolen months of her servitude and then abandoned her when it was time to pay. The world swam as her eyes filled with hot, angry tears. Angry tears that swallowed the despairing ones. She rubbed them all violently away with her palms and found that the world still wavered.

Everything had changed. The trees shimmered with transparency beneath a cold and distant sun and the ever-chirping birds were silenced. Since the click in the lock, there had been no earthly sound, not even from the wind or the deer that bounded past. She reached out her hand to touch one as it leapt, but it was nothing more than mist in her hand. Were they ghosts? Or was she?

Warm arms encircled her waist, and familiar lips brushed her hair. She turned and saw him, for the first time since the hunting accident that was no accident. The witch had kept her end of the bargain. She had given her a day with her lost love.

"Harper ..."

"Iris, how?"

Instead of explaining, she kissed him. Maybe next year, she'd tell him about the witch and the magic that joined them between worlds. Maybe the year after that, she'd tell him how she'd defied her father and refused Prince Edgar's proposal. And maybe the year after that, she'd tell him about how she'd left the castle, spitting in the face of the king and father that had murdered her love.

But here, now, in this place between living and dying, there was no room for that. No room for bitterness or rage. No room for the old roles of princess and pauper. No room for regret, or even sadness. In this place, they were their truest selves. In this place, there was room only for love.

And that was how Iris spent her longest day, loving and being loved.

The phantom sun set, washing the sky with orange and pink until it deepened to the purple of a summer night. Iris clung to Harper's hands, gazing into his eyes as he faded away and the forest returned to normal. When the evening's first stars had taken the place of his eyes, she dropped her empty hands and returned to the hut.

The Wood-Witch, rocking by the fire, smiled ruefully at her. "I expect you'll be leaving in the morning?"

Iris was surprised out of her sadness. "What? No. I started in winter, I owe you more days."

"Most of you leave once you get what you want."

"I wouldn't do that. And besides what about the spell?"

"Oh, I usually snip the strings once the silly girl runs off. I don't want a lying ninny bound to me. I'm better than that." The old woman waved the fireplace poker like a magic wand. "So, you're free! No worries—I shan't roast you in my oven. And, besides, aren't you tired of working? Don't you miss the castle? The jewels? The parties?"

Iris almost snorted. *Do I miss the prison? The fools? The betrayals?* "I promised you 364 days, and I mean to give them to you. If, after that, you'd like to dismiss me, you may. But I'll tell you now, I'd rather stay on."

The Wood-Witch swiveled in her chair, gently stirring the dying embers. Iris could have sworn she heard her mumble something about responsibility over riches.

"What did you say?"

"I said, that cauldron is not going to clean itself." This time, Iris caught the scrub brush.

The months passed happily for Iris. She gained a greater understanding of the witch's craft as she watched her. She began to see the things that cannot be seen—the Shades, the moods, the fears, the dreams. As she began to see these things, she also began to see the Wood-Witch more clearly. Most saw her as a wishing well or an evil, gnarled crone—but she was neither of those things. She was a gruff old woman, but also a brilliant artist, weaving creations of healing and magic for those in need.

It was autumn when Prince Edgar arrived. Iris was washing dishes, daydreaming about the Summer Solstice, when he galloped up on his oversized charger.

"You've got company, Princess." The Wood-Witch smirked from her rocking chair. "Quite a handsome fellow. Very princely."

"How did he find me here?" Iris threw her rag into the sink, with enough force to send dishwater and bubbles raining down on her head. She brushed them away impatiently. "I despise him."

"Oh, I know, mortal boys are so overrated. You prefer otherworldly lovers—not as much impertinence."

Iris watched in irritation as Edgar dismounted and marched towards the door, which he proceeded to kick in with unnecessary violence. He put his hands on his hips and puffed out his chest, awaiting a Hero's Welcome. When it didn't come, he grabbed Iris by the wrist and began pulling her roughly towards the door. She recoiled. "Iris, quickly. Come with me," he grunted in frustration.

The Wood-Witch stood. The air around her crackled like lightning from a storm cloud, but he didn't seem to notice. "I'm thinking the girl doesn't want to go with you."

"I don't!" Iris shouted. Right in his princely face.

"I'm rescuing you, girl," he thundered. "You must be

bewitched. No matter, we'll remedy that soon enough."
He grabbed the witch by the throat and slammed her
against the wall. His other hand reached for the dagger
at his belt.

Iris's palms began to itch, right where the witch had
sewn the invisible threads so long ago. She had been
the woman's hands long enough that she knew what to
do. She sprinted towards the cauldron and filled it with
intangible things: a crow's caw that cut the air, the hunger of the fox that hunted the woods, the sharp intake
of breath that filled the witch's lungs.

As the cauldron hissed, dense grey smoke poured
forth and rolled over the neatly swept floor. When
it reached Edgar's ankles, he released the witch and
looked about him in confusion. He stumbled to the
door, and Iris pushed him through it.

"Never come back!" she shouted.

"I'll never come back," the prince responded, his
voice docile and disoriented.

"And tell my father I wasn't here. That you couldn't
find me."

He bowed stiffly, in bewildered acquiescence. "I
will." Then he mounted his horse and galloped off into
the darkened wood.

The Wood-Witch smiled softly. "Well, Princess, you're three for three. Brains, commitment, and the desire to rescue rather than be rescued."

"Please, stop calling me Princess." The word was like a pinch.

"What shall I call you then? Apprentice?"

Iris pretended to think it over. "Do I get a day off?"

"Certainly. Which day would you like? Tomorrow, I suppose?"

"Oh, no. I choose the longest day. I choose the Summer Solstice."

J.G. Formato is a writer and elementary school teacher from North Florida. Her short fiction has appeared in a variety of venues including *Persistent Visions*, *Luna Station Quarterly*, and *Syntax & Salt Magazine*, as well as the previous Fairy Tale Villains Reimagined anthology, *Giants and Ogres*.